Knot a Clue

A Southern Quilting Mystery, Volume 13

Elizabeth Craig

Published by Elizabeth Spann Craig, 2020.

KNOT A CLUE

First edition. September 1, 2020.

Written by Elizabeth Craig.

Chapter One

Beatrice smiled as Wyatt opened the door to the backyard and came toward her with a tray holding a couple of plates heaped with breakfast food and coffees, setting them on the round table in front of her.

"Can we do this every morning?" she murmured as she saw the scrambled eggs, sausage, and pancakes.

Wyatt chuckled. "I'm not sure I'll be that motivated."

"Then I'll make sure to especially enjoy this," said Beatrice, digging into her food.

It was early fall and the yard was still beautiful from the summer. The air was cool but not chilly and Beatrice was wearing a light sweater. Wyatt had woken especially early to get ready to go to the church office and make breakfast, and it was only a little after seven now. The sun was just rising and the whole backyard glowed with early-morning light.

"Mm, this is all wonderful," said Beatrice. "Is the food from the farmer's market?"

"It's all farm-to-table, locally-sourced, and organic." Wyatt grinned at her.

They sat quietly outside, enjoying the sounds of the birds chirping at the feeders, the smell of their food and coffees, and the sun creeping over the lawn.

"What does your day look like?" asked Beatrice lazily. "Anything big going on?"

"It should be pretty quiet. No hospital visits. Nothing planned on the calendar. I'm hoping I can get some work done on my sermon."

Beatrice quirked an eyebrow at him. "From what I remember, you're about a month ahead on your sermons. Maybe two." Wyatt was a Presbyterian minister, the third generation in his family to preach at his church, Dappled Hills Presbyterian. His serious work ethic occasionally made Beatrice sigh, but she knew what a wonderful impact he made on their community. And she loved the church and its congregation. It was the kind of place where, when you walked in, you felt at home. Wyatt was much of the reason why you did.

Wyatt grinned at her, eyes crinkling in the way she loved. "Just the same, I like to have a little bit of a buffer. You know, in case anything comes up."

Beatrice finished one of the sausage links and took a sip of her coffee. "That's very optimistic of you, thinking that something exciting might come up. Lately, our excitement has consisted of winning at Scrabble with Meadow and Ramsay and introducing Will to grits."

Wyatt smiled again at the memory. Their grandbaby, Will, had decided that grits were a lot more interesting than he'd first thought. "Well, I guess excitement in Dappled Hills is relative." He gave Beatrice a curious look. "You don't ever pine for everything you used to do in Atlanta? Concerts, shows? Fancy restaurants?"

Beatrice had retired as an art museum curator in the big city to move to the mountain village of Dappled Hills; at the time, to be closer to her daughter, Piper. It was here that she met and married Wyatt.

"Not a bit," she said firmly.

Beatrice's phone rang and she frowned as she glanced at it. "That's Piper." She glanced at her watch. "She should be at school now."

She quickly answered the phone.

"Oh, Mama," said Piper miserably, "something awful has happened."

"Not Will." Beatrice's voice was hoarse and she felt a cold shudder of fear move up her spine as she thought of the baby.

"Oh no, no," said Piper hastily. "Will is absolutely fine. He's with Meadow this morning. It's just . . . someone murdered Petunia Murray."

Beatrice remembered Piper mentioning Petunia before. "She's one of the teachers at the elementary school, isn't she?"

Piper used to also teach at the elementary school, but since her son was born, she was working in the office to have fewer hours. Meadow and Beatrice watched Will some days and picked him up from church preschool on others. "Yes." Her voice became very quiet. "I found her at her desk, slumped over, right before all the kids came in. It looked like someone had hit her over the head with a globe."

Beatrice stood up and Wyatt did, too, worried furrows on his forehead. "Are you okay? Can I come pick you up?"

to say good morning to Petunia." He stopped and then started again. "At first, I couldn't tell what was wrong. I thought she'd maybe fallen back asleep at her desk, although she's always seemed like a morning person. Then I realized how awkward she looked." He turned to Piper. "And then you came in."

Piper nodded miserably. "I was doing the same as you—just stopping by to say hi to her." Her voice grew low since there were still some parents hovering around to try to find out news.

Beatrice noticed that the muscle in Fletcher's jaw twitched again. "There's no way that was a natural death. Somebody had it in for her."

"But who?" Piper shook her head, a bewildered expression on her face. "It just doesn't make any sense. Who would do something like that to a sweet elementary school teacher?"

Fletcher pressed his lips together. Then he said, "I'm not saying I know anything. All I know is that I *suspect* things."

Piper leaned in. "Was someone upset with Petunia?"

He shrugged. "I don't know for sure. But I do know Sterling Wade was very interested in Petunia. Romantically, that is."

"But she didn't feel the same?" asked Beatrice.

"Definitely not," said Fletcher dismissively. "She was way out of his league. Not that Sterling was intuitive enough to pick up on that. He was completely obsessed with her. I was going to have words with the principal about it, actually because I didn't think it was healthy for a school environment to have a fifth-grade teacher batting his eyes at another teacher. It certainly wasn't professional of him. He was always sort of lurking around Petunia. I thought it was really inappropriate. I mean, it's one thing if you're romantically pursuing someone after school hours, but it's another if it's while you're at work."

Beatrice said, "Especially if he wasn't being encouraged to do so."

"Exactly. Petunia was just being way too nice to him. I told her she should just tell him she wasn't interested."

"But she wouldn't?" asked Beatrice.

"She didn't want to hurt his feelings," said Fletcher with a short laugh. "That's the kind of person she was." He glanced at his watch. "I'd better run. I'd texted my wife to let her know what happened and she's been texting me and I really need to fill her in. Later."

He strode briskly off, gym whistle bobbing as he went.

Piper looked after him, brow puckered. "You know, we should probably leave too, Mama. Maybe you could swing by Meadow's house and I could pick the baby up and bring him back home?"

Beatrice said, "Now, Piper, why do you want to do that? You're still looking pretty shaky. I think it would be best if you and I go grab some breakfast somewhere. Maybe at June Bug's bakery? You might feel better after some coffee and one of her bacon, egg, and cheese biscuits. Besides, you know how Meadow loves spending time with Will. That will give her the chance to get her baby fix before you take him back home. Or, better yet, you go home after breakfast and put your feet up while Meadow watches him."

"You're right. I could use the break and I don't think Meadow would appreciate me pulling the plug on her time with Will yet. Plus, I really should get back in touch with Ash and give him an update on what happened."

Piper was fumbling with her phone as they walked slowly to Beatrice's car. On the way, Georgia, a fellow member of the Village Quilters guild and a teacher at the school, hurried to join them.

Georgia's pretty face was pale and her eyes cloudy as she looked at Piper. "Oh, Piper, I heard you were the one who found Petunia. I'm so sorry!" She gave her friend a quick hug.

Piper said, "Fletcher and I were the first ones on the scene. I feel awful for Petunia. She was so young and such a hard worker. I thought she was really good for the kids, too. They thought she was amazing. They're going to miss her so much." She swallowed hard.

Georgia nodded, her sweet features worried. "And she was doing so well despite the fact it was her first year at the school. I just can't believe this happened." She turned to Beatrice. "And you knew her too, didn't you? From church?"

Beatrice stopped walking. "Piper mentioned the same thing, that she went to our church." She flushed. "I'm terrible at names, but in my defense, it's tough when there are so many active members of the congregation."

Piper said, "And she was new here, so she hasn't been attending for very long."

Beatrice said slowly, "Piper, you mentioned she was blonde with colorful clothes. You know, I do think I've seen someone like that with Dora maybe." Dora was an uber-volunteer at the church—one of those women that the church absolutely depended on to keep running smoothly each week. She was also organizing a quilt show with Beatrice, although Dora was putting in most of the work.

Georgia's phone rang and she glanced at the screen. "My phone is blowing up with all my parents calling me. I'd better head back home and start calling folks back. See you two later." And she headed off to the bike rack where her bicycle was kept.

Chapter Two

A few minutes later, Beatrice pulled into a parking spot outside the bakery. There were plenty of other people who apparently had the same idea and the shop was bustling. June Bug was bustling too, but gave them a big smile when they came in. She was another member of the Village Quilters guild and quite a creative one. Beatrice had been amazed at what she could accomplish out of scraps and many of her quilts looked as if they could easily gain admittance to folk art museums. But June Bug, quiet, shy, and always busy, couldn't be less interested in recognition for what she considered a relaxing hobby . . . although Beatrice had tried to convince her otherwise.

They placed their orders at the counter and then Beatrice and Piper sat down and chatted a little while June Bug put the orders together and helped other customers. Beatrice tried to keep the conversation lighter with Piper—focusing on the different projects she was doing to use up scraps, the book she was reading with Wyatt and their different takes on it, her unsuccessful attempts to resuscitate a houseplant that appeared to be in its final stages of life, and her more-successful attempts at sustaining an herb garden in the backyard.

Piper seemed to get more of her color back and laughed at all the right parts, even though she remained pretty quiet. She perked up when their breakfast sandwiches were ready and the bakery cleared out to the point June bug could trot over and spend a few minutes in conversation.

Beatrice said, "I love the quilts you put up. The whole shop feels so cheerful." The walls were draped with quilts of all different styles and in all different colors. The effect was one that was both happy and calming at the same time.

The little woman's round face flushed with pleasure. She looked around the bakery with satisfaction. "They're pretty, aren't they? The quilters were so sweet to loan them." On every quilt hanging on the walls there was a little sign explaining who the quilter was and a little bit about the quilt. The quilters had all chosen bright, colorful quilts which made the shop pop with color.

Beatrice said, "I noticed the flyers for the quilt show at your register, too. Thanks for putting those out." The quilt show was coming up and Beatrice was a co-organizer with Dora Tucker. It was a role she hadn't initially planned on taking on, but the other members of the guild had been much busier than she'd been and there hadn't really been a great excuse to turn the role down. Beatrice had generally found that she'd been just about as busy in retirement as she'd been when she worked at the museum.

June Bug's eyes crinkled in a smile. "I might need some more soon since people have been picking them up. I'll bring some back from the guild meeting." Then her face fell as she gazed sadly at Piper. "I heard the news from the school from one of the parents. I was so relieved Rowena could pick up the girls from school. Are you okay?" She looked at Piper with her large, round, bug-like eyes. Rowena was a new employee of June Bug's and was helping her out a lot, not only at the store, but by keeping an eye on her daughter and June Bug's niece from time to time.

Piper nodded quickly. "I was just really shaken up. But I'm better now. And the kids should be back in school tomorrow, I think."

The bell on the door rang and a group of women came in, chatting and laughing and talking about the different things they liked at the bakery.

"See you at the guild meeting," said June Bug, hurrying off.

"I'll bring more flyers," Beatrice called behind her.

Beatrice was just searching her mind for more banal and hopefully calming conversation topics and had settled on the surprising complications of setting up a quilt show when Piper reached out a hand to place it on hers.

"Mama, I know what you're trying to do and I really appreciate it. Now that I've had some food and a little coffee, it might help me sort things out if I actually talk about what happened. I need to get things straight in my head and talking it through should help. Plus, if I can get through the whole thing without crying, that would be great." Her eyes grew a little misty and she blinked to force the tears away.

Beatrice said warmly, "Of course we can talk about it if you're ready, sweetheart."

Piper said, "I'm just working it all out. So I had a regular morning. Up at the usual time. Managed a quick run on the treadmill before my shower. Will was sleeping in a little so I was able to get totally ready before I needed to feed and dress him. Then I got Will ready and all his baby gear and Ash took him over to his mom's house on his way to the college. And I headed over to the elementary school. I was even a few minutes early, so I thought I'd stick my head in and say good morning to Petunia on the way to the office."

Beatrice nodded. "You and she were friends."

Piper shook her head slowly. "I wouldn't say that. I feel bad now that we weren't any closer. After all, between the school and church, I saw her pretty often. I thought she seemed really sweet and she was new to the school, so I figured I'd try to make her feel welcome. The kids loved her and I wanted her to stick around. I know the first year at a new school can be tough, so I was hoping things were going well and trying to be friendly."

Beatrice said, "I wish I had more of an impression of her from church. I do know who you're talking about, but aside from realizing she was doing a good bit of volunteering and working with Dora, I didn't really know her. Where did she move from?"

"I think from somewhere in Georgia. Her parents are still living there, I know." Piper winced. "I hate that her family is going to be getting such awful news and over the phone."

Beatrice dropped her voice a little. "This whole thing seems so awful. Surely, she hadn't been here long enough to make any enemies."

Piper gave a helpless shrug. "No one I knew about. And she always looked so happy . . . she had this really sunny smile. It wasn't like she was in fear for her life." She paused. "There was one thing. I'm sure it didn't mean anything, though."

"What was it?"

Piper hesitated. "I don't know. It's just that, as much as I liked Petunia, she could come across as a bit of a flirt sometimes. I'm sure it was just her friendly nature and she didn't really realize how she appeared."

Beatrice nodded. "She was flirting with someone at the school?"

"Fletcher King. Or maybe not. Like I said, maybe it was just her way of being friendly."

Beatrice said slowly, "And Fletcher was the gym teacher we just met over at the school." She remembered his face flushing as he spoke about Petunia. And he'd been in her classroom right before Piper had gotten there.

"Exactly. Her class was in the gym for their P.E. time and I'd headed over there to deliver a message from a parent for Petunia. Neither of them saw me for about a minute and it crossed my mind that they looked a little cozy. He had his hand on her back in kind of a familiar way. It might not have meant anything at all. Maybe that was his way of just being outgoing."

Beatrice said, "Fletcher did go in to say hi to Petunia this morning. At least, that's what he said he was doing."

Piper's face was grim. "I can't imagine the elementary school gym teacher murdering anybody, especially Petunia. But you're right . . . he was in the room first and it sure seems like he was friendly with her, if nothing else."

"He didn't seem like he was big on workplace romances, though, from what he was saying to us."

Piper said, "*And* he's married. So he *really* shouldn't be into workplace romances."

"Who was it he mentioned?" asked Beatrice. "The man who might have had a crush on Petunia?"

Piper sighed. "It was Sterling Wade. I've always felt a little sorry for him. He does try really hard and his students do seem to enjoy his class. But he's so socially awkward with adults. Maybe that's why he decided to go into teaching, since he gets along so much easier with kids."

"Fletcher acted as if Sterling wasn't much of a catch."

"Well, not in Fletcher's eyes, I guess. Sterling is sort of nerdy-looking with a high forehead and big glasses. He goes to our church and helps with the children's ministry there. He gets really enthusiastic about science and does cool experiments for his fifth-graders," said Piper.

"Oh, that's why his name is familiar. He's in charge of Vacation Bible School in the summer, isn't he? But he's apparently got a few issues, too."

Piper nodded. "Exactly. He doesn't seem to really pick up on social cues easily. Fletcher was right; Petunia was way out of Sterling's league, but that didn't stop him from looking at her with big calf eyes and following her around." She sighed. "He even tried to date Georgia, back before she was seeing Tony."

Beatrice raised her eyebrows. "How did that go?"

"Not well at all. But if Tony is Georgia's type, then Sterling definitely wouldn't have been interesting to her, romantically-speaking. You know, Tony's sort of a man's man. He can make anything and fix anything. Georgia dispatched Sterling really well, though, while still leaving him his dignity. I think by the end of things, he thought he'd decided *she* wasn't right for *him*."

"Well, Georgia has always been such a kind person. I'm guessing Petunia might not have handled things the same way? Although I think Fletcher said she was 'too nice' to Sterling?"

Piper said, "Maybe she was too nice when she was dealing directly with Sterling. But when Sterling wasn't around, she'd groan over it. She mostly seemed exasperated over it all. She actually mentioned it to me briefly because she was so frustrated and wanted a little advice. Of course, I told her if Sterling was being a pest that she should speak with the school administration. I think our principal really listens to the staff and definitely wouldn't want to have any harassment going on at the school."

"But Petunia didn't want to report him to the principal?" asked Beatrice.

Piper shook her head. "No. She said she was so new at the school. Petunia felt that complaining about Sterling would make it look like she was making trouble. She also didn't want to get Sterling into any real trouble or have him lose his job. I told her I was sure the school would totally understand and would have a word with Sterling: they'd find a good way to handle it. But she was adamant she could handle it herself. Petunia almost acted like she was sorry she'd said anything to me about it."

Beatrice finished off her breakfast biscuit. "It sounds like there was definitely drama surrounding Petunia, especially for someone so new to town."

Piper smoothed a strand of dark hair away from her face. "And that's not all, although I don't really know much about what was going on with Elspeth."

"Elspeth? Not Elspeth McDonald from church?" Beatrice couldn't picture their loyal volunteer with her gray hair always pulled severely back in a bun being involved in any sort of trouble.

Piper said, "From church and school. I heard her squabbling with Petunia after school one day, but I have no idea what the problem was."

Beatrice frowned, remembering Elspeth's cheerful volunteering and her ability to keep focused and un-embroiled in the little quarrels and frays that inevitably happened in committees, even in a church community. "I wouldn't have said Elspeth was the type of person to get engaged in pointless arguments."

Piper nodded. "I know what you mean. I've always gotten along really well with Elspeth at the school. When I'd first started teaching there, she was so helpful . . . a veteran teacher taking a new one under her wing. I learned so much from her about how to engage the children and control a classroom. And I know Elspeth was acting as Petunia's mentor as well because the school had asked Elspeth to step into that role. I'm not sure what Petunia and Elspeth were quarreling about; I just know Petunia was standing there, still wearing that cute craft apron of hers, hands on her hips and frowning. But Petunia looked very concerned. And Elspeth seemed sort of defensive and frantic."

"I'm pretty sure Elspeth helps out with Wednesday nights at the church. I'll have to make sure to look out for her tonight when Wyatt and I are there. I'd love to hear her perspective on Petunia." Beatrice swirled her iced tea and the ice cubes clinked against the glass.

"If she can give it." Piper said sadly and added in a low voice, "I haven't wanted to say anything, but I've really noticed some changes with Elspeth in the last few months. She's been sort of addled lately. I mean, we're all tired at the school and we all can be absentminded, but she's taking it to another level. Maybe she has something on her mind and it's distracting her from the task at hand. But for a teacher her age who's been at the school for a million years, it's odd that her classroom has been so completely out of control. I heard some other teachers talking about her the other day—they'd had to stick their heads in and fuss at the students when they were walking by her classroom."

"Yikes," said Beatrice. "I'll check in with her tonight. Not only might she have information on Petunia, she might have some personal struggles going on that Wyatt can possibly counsel her about."

Piper looked at her watch. "Okay, I think I'm ready to get hooked back up with my car now if you'd like to drive me back to the school. Thanks so much, Mama, for this. I feel a lot better now. In fact, I think I'll take your advice and just head home and put my feet up for a little while before picking Will up from Meadow's house. But I need to call her and let her know."

Beatrice put a tip down on the table and stood up. "Nope. You'll be on the phone all day if you call her, Piper. She'll be asking dozens of questions about Petunia and fretting over the wicked state of Dappled Hills. Then she'll give you a twenty-minute breakdown of every morsel Will has consumed and all the adorable things he did in her care. I'll give her a ring and fill her in. You get your rest, sweetie."

They waved to June Bug who gave them a cheery smile as they left.

Beatrice drove Piper back to the school parking lot and gave her a hug before Piper left. She drove back to her house, figuring she could update Wyatt from there and then fill Meadow in. The thing about Meadow, as she'd told Piper, is that she could spend forever on the phone with you. But then, she did have their grandbaby at her house, so maybe she'd keep it short for once.

As Beatrice pulled into her driveway, she saw the sheer curtains in the front picture window move and Noo-noo's foxy face peering intently out to see if it was friend or foe outside. Spotting Beatrice getting out of her car, the little dog immediately started grinning.

As Beatrice came inside, the corgi started doing a skipping, hopping dance from sheer excitement, which put a smile on Beatrice's face. She plopped down on the floor with Noo-Noo to rub her for a few minutes and called Wyatt while she did to fill him in. Then, after spending seven or eight minutes on the floor, she remembered why she usually sat in a low chair when petting Noo-Noo. And why she used a little bench when she was gardening outside. Getting *on* the floor or ground was no big deal. Getting *off* the floor or ground required a bit more maneuvering.

She'd just patted herself on the back for successfully managing it when there was a knock on her door. Actually, it was more of a flurry of knocking, which could only mean one thing: Meadow Downey.

membered who she was, but I don't think I ever introduced myself to her."

Meadow waved her hand dismissively. "Beatrice, there are far too many people in and out of the church all the time for you to know all of them. I know Wyatt doesn't expect you to know them."

"But Wyatt *does* know them."

"Yes, but he's the minister! And he's been the minister there for decades. You're simply the minister's wife who's trying her very best. Besides, Petunia was new to town. Also, I think Dora considered her 'her project,' so you might not have even had the opportunity to meet Petunia."

Beatrice gave Will's soft baby hair a nuzzle and asked, "Project?"

"You know how Dora Tucker is. She likes to feel like she's in charge."

Beatrice said thoughtfully, "I sort of thought she *was* in charge. In a volunteer capacity, of course. But she's a church deacon, goes to practically every event the church offers, and runs a ton of committees. I'm not sure what the church would do without her."

Meadow said, "Yes, yes. I'm not saying that she doesn't offer a very valuable service to the church. But she is rather bossy and does sort of act like a know-it-all." She gasped and covered her mouth. "Oh, goodness. Isn't she the co-chair for the quilt show you and she are putting on?"

"She is, and I've been very relieved that she was."

Meadow asked, "Does she ever ask your opinion about anything? Or does she just take over the whole thing?"

"She doesn't really ask my opinion until after it's already done. Dora came up with the flyers to advertise the show and she asked what I thought of them . . . I guess as a sort of courtesy. But if I *hadn't* liked them, we just would have been out of luck because she'd already printed up a slew of flyers," said Beatrice.

Meadow wagged her finger. "That's exactly what I'm talking about. What if there'd been a typo or something on there? What if she'd left out the date or the location of the event?"

Beatrice shook her head. "Dora Tucker isn't the sort of person to do that. She probably proofread it a million times. Like I said, she's so in-charge that I really haven't had to do much to prepare for the show. I'll just show up, help organize the quilt exhibits, and clean up." She paused. "What does Dora have to do with Petunia again? I've gotten turned around."

"Well, first off they're neighbors. Dora apparently took it upon herself to act as the welcoming committee for her neighborhood. Then she asked Petunia if she'd found a church home. She hadn't of course, since she'd just moved in a couple of days before, so Dora invited her to come to church with her . . . probably quite a few times until she wore down any resistance Petunia might have had. Then she got her to come with her to Wednesday nights and her Bible study on Thursdays. Like I said, Petunia has definitely been at the church, but she's been kept busy. No wonder you haven't had a chance to meet her."

Will curiously took a handful of Beatrice's hair, wrapping his small hand in the platinum-gray strands and Beatrice gave him another snuggle, making him giggle. She loved the baby smell of him.

"What else do you know about Petunia?" asked Beatrice. "Anything that might explain what happened to her?"

Meadow shook her head angrily. "No. The very idea of this happening at a *school* in Dappled Hills! I simply cannot fathom. What is this world coming to?"

"Did you hear about Petunia having any relationships?" asked Beatrice.

Meadow looked thoughtful. "No, but then I didn't really know Petunia. Although there was something a couple of weeks ago that surprised me, now that you mention it. I saw Petunia over at Fletcher King's house. You know how he's our new neighbor in that little house that's set back from the road?"

"Are you sure it was Petunia?"

"Absolutely. She was very distinctive: always wearing primary colors that set off her blonde hair. The kids must have loved her cheery outfits. Anyway, she stood out. It was most definitely Petunia. It gave me pause for a moment, but then I remembered that of course they were both working at the same school. I figured it must have been some sort of school-related errand that brought Petunia there." But Meadow's face was doubtful.

Beatrice said, "And I know Fletcher isn't single."

"No. No, he has a wife named Edie. That's what was really so startling. I brought Edie a bunch of food when they moved in. She's a Realtor so I had to make sure her car was there when I dropped everything off because she might have been out showing homes."

"What's Edie like?" asked Beatrice.

Meadow shrugged. "She's okay. Honestly, she was a little off-putting that day, but I suppose she might have been in the middle of something when I showed up. But I couldn't exactly have called ahead when I didn't have their number. And I was just trying to be neighborly." Meadow's voice was now getting a tinge of defensiveness in it.

"Was she actively rude then?" asked Beatrice, surprised. Because when faced with a cornucopia of Meadow's excellent cooking, it was hard to imagine someone being rude.

"No, not *really*. She just looked stressed, mainly. And she kept looking at the boxes when I was talking to her as if she couldn't wait to get rid of me so she could keep unpacking."

Beatrice frowned. "I'm just surprised I haven't seen her. I've noticed Fletcher, but never realized he had a wife until Piper told me about her."

"Brown hair, shoulder-length. Big glasses. Looks smart."

Beatrice said slowly, "Now I feel like I've seen her at church and not on our street."

Meadow clapped her hands, which startled Will. She rubbed his back absently and said, "Yes, she *has* been at church. In fact, she's helping out with the music there—filling in when the music director is out. She just started a few weeks ago, I think. So I guess she has two jobs: one in real estate and one at the church. No wonder you haven't seen her around the neighborhood."

"I remember her now. And I remember Wyatt saying they were lucky to have her; she's apparently very good and can play several instruments." Beatrice decided that maybe she'd try to catch up with Edie as well as Elspeth at the church that night. It was starting to sound like a busy evening.

"Something about Petunia's death?" asked Beatrice soberly.

Meadow said, "What? No. No, I found out that Dora has *plans* for the quilt show. Beatrice, she really must be stopped."

Beatrice slumped. "The idea of stopping Dora from doing anything really doesn't appeal. She's a force of nature. Besides, what sort of radical plans could Dora possibly have for the quilt show?"

"The fact she hasn't even gone over them with you should tell us something. You're the co-planner! And you're absolutely right: 'radical' is precisely the right word for her ideas."

"The plans, Meadow?" prompted Beatrice. She looked longingly at the quilt fabric across the room.

"Oh, right. She wants to skip the cake sale! Can you believe it?" Meadow huffed indignantly.

This actually was something of a surprise. The cake sale always sold out and had proven a reliable way of raising money for the guilds: either for future shows or their charitable outreach in the community. And the cakes were all from June Bug, which meant they were absolutely amazing. They sold them by the slice and it was one of the few times she made her famous but complicated toffee apple cake. "Did she say why?"

Meadow snorted. "Well, she told June Bug that she wanted to go with something more substantial for the food sale." She paused for effect and then said, voice dripping with displeasure, "Sandwiches! With individual bags of chips."

Beatrice mulled this over. "That will mean we'll probably have to provide more beverages, too. Chips are salty and the sandwiches might be, too."

"I say we don't accept it! That we rebel against the plan. There's something important about tradition, don't you think? And those cakes are practically the only way I can get Ramsay to *go* to his umpteenth quilt show and probably most of the other men, too. He sure isn't going to be excited about showing up for chips and a sandwich. Or the *rock music*."

"Rock music?" Beatrice's lips twitched at Meadow's tone. She was no longer trying to keep her voice low. For her own safety, she hoped Dora Tucker wouldn't happen into the bakery.

"I know! The very idea. We always pipe in folk music or jazz to the shows. She's proposing some sort of live music. It would be awful. Why on earth distract from the quilts, which is the whole reason we're there? I bet it's all nepotism. She probably has a nephew or something that has a garage band."

Beatrice couldn't see it, but she had the distinct impression Meadow shuddered.

"Tell you what—I'll speak with Dora. I can't make any promises, though, since I'm not sure my opinion really holds a lot of weight with her. But I'll be sure to voice your concerns."

Will started fussing in the background and Meadow quickly said, "Better go. I think someone needs a diaper change."

Beatrice hung up with a sense of relief. She fixed herself a snack and another coffee and immediately settled in with her latest series of small quilting projects. She'd decided she had so many scraps that it might be best for her to just use some of the fabric up before starting something new. She'd had something of a creative block for a little while . . . she'd also been busy sharing babysitting responsibilities with Meadow for Will. Then a simple project had gotten her back on track. The lack of quilting was also a reason she'd gotten involved with organizing the quilt show. Beatrice had figured that being active with the guild might help jump-start her quilting again.

Now she was busily working through small projects to use up the old scraps. First, she'd organized the scraps by color and had tossed any fabric pieces she didn't really love. This took a long while to do and several times during the process she wondered if she'd lost her mind. But when she was done, she had so many ideas when she looked at the carefully-sorted piles of cloth. She had so many different fabric patterns, too: florals, batiks, geometrics, and traditional. She'd made change purses (they were going to be on sale at the quilt show), bibs (Will was still a rather enthusiastic eater), pincushions, coffee table quilts, and quilted placemats.

After working for about an hour, Beatrice glanced at the clock. She still had some free time to relax before heading off to church for the Wednesday night gathering. And if approaching Dora about the show was on the agenda, she was going to need that free time to relax before trying to beard the lion. Beatrice was reading a Golden Age mystery, Margery Allingham's *The Crime at Black Dudley*, which was giving her chills. It was a country house mystery involving a very odd game and it was absorbing enough to pull her right into the story.

Noo-noo snuggled up with her on the sofa, making little snorting sounds as she tried to get herself as close as possible to Beatrice and then fell promptly asleep, snoring gently, as Beatrice read. It was a long time before she looked at her watch again and when she did, she was surprised to see it was *past* time for her to be at the church. She quickly got up, changed her clothes to something a little more minister's-wife-ish, and quickly touched up her makeup. Then she walked over since the church was right down the street and it had stopped raining.

She entered the fellowship hall where the church served supper in a buffet line. The church had redecorated the hall a few years earlier and it was a much warmer-looking room than the one it had been. Thin carpeting in a gray and brown pattern covered the floor and there was a lot more lighting from wrought-iron chandeliers. Wyatt smiled at her, excused himself from the group he was speaking to, and came over to give her a hug. "How did everything go with Piper this morning? Is she all right now?"

"She's fine and is back home with Will," said Beatrice. She lowered her voice, "Since Petunia Murray attended church here, I thought you should know she's the one who died this morning."

Wyatt's eyes grew wide. "Oh no. Yes, I know exactly who she is—she was speaking to me just recently about taking the new member class soon. I'm so sorry to hear that." He paused. "Does she have any family here in town? I should speak with them."

Beatrice said, "I'm not sure, although it sounds as if she was here in town by herself. I believe someone said she had family in Georgia. Apparently, Dora was spending some time showing her around the church?"

Wyatt nodded absently, a furrow between his brows. "I remember Dora telling me that she was introducing Petunia around and helping to get her involved in church. I'll call up Ramsay tomorrow and see if he can help me reach out to Petunia's family."

Edgenora's face became serious. "Is it about Petunia Murray's death? I was so sorry to hear about that. That poor young woman."

"It sounds like the news is spreading fast," said Beatrice. "You'd think I'd be used to that by now, but it's always a surprise how quickly news travels in Dappled Hills."

Edgenora said, "Does Wyatt know? That was something else on my list of things to speak with him about."

"Yes, actually, I just told him. He knew someone had died at the school this morning, but he didn't know who it was until just now. Actually, I wanted to ask you something else, though it might be somewhat related. I heard that Elspeth McDonald might be having a few issues lately. Do you know anything about that?"

"You mean memory issues?" asked Edgenora immediately.

Beatrice's heart sank a little. Of all the health problems to have, she felt memory loss was the cruelest. "It's true, then?"

"I'm afraid so. At least, that's what I understand. We've been trying to protect Elspeth from running into problems here at the church because she's still in that stage where any lapses are very worrisome to her."

"How is everyone protecting her?"

"Well, for one thing, Elspeth was running the Wednesday night women's Bible study, but there was a sort of a gentle coup to replace her. She was getting so befuddled that they would sometimes study the same Bible chapter more than once. Or, worse, Elspeth would show up without any notes at all. Occasionally, she'd forget to come to church completely. That works all right for serving food in the fellowship hall, but it's not as good when it comes to leading a Bible study," said Edgenora.

"How did the group handle the leadership change?"

Edgenora said, "I thought it was done very well. They spoke to Wyatt about it before they did anything, just to sort of get his perspective on how best to manage it. And you know how kind Wyatt is."

Beatrice nodded. Wyatt's kindness, patience, and thoughtfulness always amazed her . . . and made her a little envious. She kept trying to improve, but sometimes it wasn't easy to remember when she was in the middle of a frustrating event.

Edgenora continued, "So they did it really well, I thought. They told Elspeth that Peggy Major had been dying to lead Bible study on Wednesday nights but she wasn't sure how to go about it . . . that she was anxious about it and wondered if she'd be a good fit. A member of the group asked Elspeth if she would allow Peggy to be an apprentice for her and give her some tips."

Beatrice smiled. "That sounds like a good way to approach it."

"Karen from the group told me that it worked *so* well. She said Elspeth was proud and pleased as punch. Plus, Karen said she thought Elspeth seemed *very* relieved."

Beatrice said, "It must be very stressful to try to keep up with everything and she has such a busy life! She's an elementary school teacher and then she does a lot of things over here, too."

"I know. I was wondering how things were going at school for her. Then I figured that maybe Elspeth was so worn out from holding it all together at school that things just sort of fell apart for church. She's always been so organized that I really feel for her."

Beatrice said, "I wonder if she's thinking about retirement at all. She must have been teaching for forever." She hesitated telling Edgenora about Elspeth's possible problems teaching, feeling she didn't need to spread gossip.

"Thirty years, is what Elspeth told me once." Edgenora glanced across the room and said, "I'd better run, Beatrice. I see someone over there I need to speak with about the church yoga class." And she quickly hurried away.

A group of ladies came up and chatted to Beatrice for a few minutes about a new program the church had before heading for the buffet line. Before Beatrice could join them, a voice spoke behind her.

"Mrs. Thompson?"

She turned to see a man in his 30s with wavy hair and black-framed glasses. "Beatrice, please," she said automatically. "I think you're Sterling?"

He looked pleased to be recognized. "That's right." He suddenly jutted out a hand. "Good to finally meet you. I work with your daughter, Piper, at the elementary school." He paused. "That's why I wanted to ask you how she's doing—because I know what happened this morning. I thought about calling her this afternoon, but then I didn't want to bother her. I thought maybe she might be taking a nap or something after having such a rough morning."

Piper was right—he was very awkward, at least around other adults. She smiled reassuringly at him, hoping to put him more at ease. "That's very kind of you to ask after her. I think she might have put her feet up for a while this morning, but then she picked Will up so all prospects of napping were probably off at that point. She's doing all right, but of course it was a terrible shock. And poor Petunia."

To Beatrice's alarm, Sterling immediately teared up, which he apologized for as he fiercely blinked his eyes to dispel the tears. "I'm sorry. Sorry." He removed his glasses and scrubbed quickly at his eyes with the palm of his hand before putting his glasses back on.

Beatrice reached out to give his arm a squeeze. "Don't apologize, Sterling. You must have considered Petunia a friend, having worked with her at the school. And you probably knew her from here at church, too? I know she was becoming very involved here."

He nodded miserably and sniffed a couple of times as Beatrice dug around in her purse for her pack of tissues. She found them after pawing past a lipstick, a change purse, and a tin of mints and proffered the pack to Sterling, which he accepted gratefully. After blowing his nose, he said quietly, "Petunia was one of the reasons I became more involved in church recently. That's probably a terrible thing to say since I know my motivation should have been loftier. Now I'm totally invested in helping here no matter what. I'm really excited about some of the things we're going to implement for the kids on Sunday nights and next summer at Vacation Bible School. But originally, I'll admit that I thought volunteering here might be a good way to see Petunia outside of work."

Beatrice remembered Piper saying Sterling might have been a little too determined in his pursuit of Petunia. "I've heard that

Dora was doing a great job introducing Petunia to people at the church and getting her involved in different ways here."

Now a look of exasperation passed over Sterling's features. "That's right. Although I thought Dora kept Petunia *too* busy, frankly. I mean, it was nice of her to help her meet new people and get involved in various groups, of course. But Petunia already had a very full schedule with teaching and grading and then Dora really heaped onto that."

"Perhaps Petunia didn't mind staying busy," said Beatrice mildly.

Sterling shrugged. "Maybe." He brooded for a minute over his lack of romantic opportunity with Petunia and then teared up again. "Sorry," he blurted again as he took another tissue from the pack and swabbed his face with it. "Maybe I shouldn't have come tonight, but I thought I'd go a little crazy at home thinking about things. And I wanted to talk to Piper, too—I thought maybe she'd be at church tonight."

Beatrice shook her head. "I think she decided to stay at home and turn in early. That's just my guess. What was it that you wanted to speak with her about? I did talk with her for a little while when I picked her up from the school."

"She saw her, right? Petunia? That's what the other teachers were saying."

Beatrice nodded and Sterling took a deep, shuddering breath. He continued, "Did she think Petunia suffered? I just couldn't stand it if she did. It's bad enough that she's gone. If I thought that she'd been hurting and scared and alone on top of it?" He shook his head.

Beatrice said quickly, "Probably Ramsay Downey is the one to ask about that, although I'm not sure he'll be at the church tonight, under the circumstances. But from what little I've heard, I can't imagine she did. She likely never knew what hit her."

Sterling slumped with relief. "Yes. That's what I hoped." He looked blankly across the room and added, "I just keep thinking that if I'd been there just a little bit earlier, I could have stopped it. If I hadn't been running late this morning." His voice was filled with anger and bitterness.

"You shouldn't think that way, Sterling. There was probably nothing you could have done if someone was truly bent on ending Petunia's life. Perhaps you'd have even become a victim, yourself, in the process of trying to help."

Sterling gave her a small smile. "Thanks. It was just such a crazy morning this morning. Nothing was going right. I spilled hot coffee all over myself at breakfast and had to change clothes again before leaving the house. Then I had a nail in my tire and had to put on the spare. After that, I realized I had dirt and grease all over my clothes and had to go home to change *again*." He shook his head. "That's why I think if everything had gone according to plan, maybe I'd have been able to make a difference to the outcome."

Beatrice said, "That must feel very frustrating. It seems you and Petunia were becoming close."

Sterling looked pleased, bouncing lightly in place. "You could say so. It was a burgeoning relationship, at any rate. I made her a playlist just last week with some of my favorite songs.

There was a small age difference between us, but I thought she'd enjoy hearing some new music."

Beatrice smiled sympathetically at him although her mind was thinking he sounded very much like a middle schooler with a crush. And there was more than a small age difference between Petunia and Sterling. It was far more like a middle-sized age difference. Petunia was in her twenties from what she'd gathered and Sterling was in his early-to-mid thirties.

He said, "I've been wracking my brains trying to figure out who might have done this. I mean, who could *possibly* have had anything against Petunia? She was . . . perfect. Absolutely perfect. Besides, she was new to town—how could she have gotten on anyone's bad side in such a short time? And it's not as if there was a robbery or something involved. I've heard through the grapevine that her purse wasn't even touched. It sounds like it was something personal, but it's so hard to come up with what."

"Did you have any ideas who might be involved?"

He shook his head, making a face. "Who would do something like that?" He paused, glancing across the room at the buffet line where Elspeth was doling out tacos, her hair pulled back into its usual severe bun and her trademark red lipstick turning her mouth into a bold ribbon. "I can't imagine even *her* doing something like that."

Beatrice followed his gaze. "You mean Elspeth?"

"She and Petunia argued last week, that's all. It was after school one day." He continued watching Elspeth from across the room. "And I really do like Elspeth. We go to community events together every once in a while."

Beatrice asked, "Did you hear what the argument was about?"

"No, they stopped when I came into the room. All I know is that I heard their raised voices from down the hall. And, when I came in the room, I could see Petunia was in tears." He brightened for a moment at a happier memory. "I brought Petunia flowers the next day since she'd had such a rough time the day before. She seemed very excited about them."

Beatrice felt again the sensation that this infatuation resembled a youthful crush. "I'm sure she appreciated that."

He nodded and then said, "Well, I'd better head on. I'm leading the Bible study again for my group and I need to get into the classroom early to set things up. I have a slideshow to prepare on Jeremiah." He gave her a shy smile and scampered off.

Beatrice stood in the buffet line and had her tacos, Mexican rice, and corn salad heaped on her plate by Elspeth and the other ladies. Elspeth gave her a warm smile but Beatrice knew better than to try to really speak with her there. Instead, she took her plate to one of the tables and sat with a family she knew. She ate while Wyatt, back from his meeting, introduced the Wednesday night speaker: a guest minister who was also an expert in family relationships. At one point, Beatrice glanced over to see Elspeth finishing up with serving the tacos and heading off to the fellowship hall kitchen to clean up. As soon as the speaker wrapped up, Beatrice headed back to the kitchen, too.

Beatrice cleared her throat so as not to startle Elspeth, who was carefully loading the industrial dishwasher with serving plates and spoons. Elspeth, deep in her thoughts, didn't notice and so Beatrice softly called out her name. She spun around, startled, putting a hand to her chest.

"I'm so sorry," said Beatrice, giving her an apologetic smile. "I just wanted to speak to you for a minute since there was no way to chat in the serving line . . . I didn't mean to startle you."

Elspeth gave her a warm smile in return. "That's all right, Beatrice. It's always good to talk with you."

Beatrice looked at the pots in the sink and said, "How about if I wash and you dry? Unless you want to put these in the dish-washer, too?"

"No, I usually do handwash the pots," said Elspeth, looking pleased. "They take up so much room and I never feel all the food comes off them in the dishwasher."

Beatrice started scrubbing the pots. "How are you doing?" asked Beatrice, glancing sideways at Elspeth. "I know you had an unexpected day off today with everything going on at the school."

Elspeth nodded sadly, her face troubled. "I'm afraid so. I guess your daughter filled you in. Yes, such a terrible thing. The poor young woman, still with so much life ahead of her. It's just a terrible shame. It pained me to hear about it."

Beatrice said, "Were you already at the school when it happened?"

"Goodness, no. I've been teaching for too many years to rise before the chickens. No, I have my routine down to a science now."

Elspeth proceeded to recite it to Beatrice: the morning stretching, the getting dressed, the feeding of the cat, the Bible study time with her coffee, as if proud of remembering and relating it all.

"That's probably just as well," said Beatrice. "I'm sure it would have been very upsetting to be at the school with all the emergency vehicles. Did you know Petunia well? It's not a very big school, I know."

Elspeth immediately shook her head. "No, I didn't really know her at all. I suppose I should have reached out to her more, as a new teacher at the school, but you know how it is: you get into your own little world. I wouldn't have really had any cause to work closely with her, of course, since she was a younger teacher."

But Beatrice saw Elspeth's face flush at the lie. Clearly, Elspeth knew Petunia a bit more than she was letting on. Piper had said Elspeth was Petunia's mentor teacher which meant she certainly had spent some time with her to help advise her and likely help Petunia develop her curriculum.

"And you didn't know her from church at all?" she asked lightly. "It's just you're so involved over here and I know Petunia was becoming very involved, too."

"Not from church, no," said Elspeth briskly. Then she hesitated. "Although, of course, I know exactly who Petunia *was*. And I did hear her having a very lively argument with Dora Tucker right here in the fellowship hall not long ago."

Chapter Five

"An argument?"

"Yes. I didn't think Dora was acting very Christian, actually." Elspeth pinkened some more, this time with indignation.

"Could you tell what the argument was about?" asked Beatrice.

Elspeth concentrated on her drying. "Of course, I was *trying* not to listen in because I certainly wouldn't have wanted to be accused of eavesdropping. But I did pick up a thread of it." She pressed her lips tightly shut before hurrying on. "You'll have to speak to Dora about it if you want to know what was said, though. It's not my place to say anything."

Beatrice nodded and decided a change of subject was definitely in order. Elspeth seemed rattled and, more than that, agitated. She said soothingly, "Well, it all must have been very upsetting. Why don't you tell me more about how *you're* doing?" Beatrice pulled a long-ago bit of conversation out of her brain and asked, "And your daughter?"

Elspeth looked pleased again as she vigorously rubbed a large pot with a towel. "Jane's doing well." Then she gave a flustered laugh. "Actually, I suppose she would say she's *not* doing well. She's just gone through a divorce, although it was a fairly simple one since they had no children. But the wonderful part about it all is that she decided to move to Dappled Hills. She wants a fresh start in a new place. And all I keep thinking about is how wonderful it will be to have her around again. We can have lunches together and spend time on the weekends. I can bring her to church and introduce her around." She stopped drying the pot she was working on and smiled at her thoughts. "I'll have to help her find a place to live. Of course, she can live with me while she's looking. That will be lovely, too."

Beatrice rinsed off a pot and gently handed it to Elspeth to dry. "That *will* be wonderful. I'm so happy for you, Elspeth. I did sort of the same thing myself when I left Atlanta to move here and be closer to Piper. I've loved every minute of it."

Elspeth said, "By the way, I saw the flyers for the quilt show. I was thinking about going, if I can."

"You should—it's a nice way to spend a day. We'll have food there and there'll be lots of folks from around town. And the quilts are always spectacular. Have you done any quilting, yourself?"

Elspeth shook her head. "Not quilting, no. But I've always admired it and love seeing all the different designs. I used to be crafty, though, a long time ago." She looked a little wistful.

"What kinds of crafts did you do?"

Elspeth said, "Oh, this and that. A bit of knitting, scrapbooking, needlepoint. It was a nice way of staying busy when I had a small child around."

"Have you thought about picking it back up again?" asked Beatrice.

"Goodness, no. I mean, I'd love to, but between teaching school and doing things here at church, I just don't have the time."

Beatrice said in a carefully casual way, "That's a pity, but I totally understand. When I was working, I didn't have any time at all to do *anything*. I'd come home completely tapped-out at the end of the day."

Elspeth nodded, sympathetically. "That's exactly the way I am now. Except I make myself go back out again on Wednesday nights to church, of course. But most every other day, I'm on my sofa as soon as I get back home from school."

"Since I've been retired, though, I've had so much more time to explore different things. I go on hikes with Wyatt and read books I never had time to read. I do some gardening and quilting, too. Have you thought about retiring?"

Elspeth nodded again, looking thoughtful. "I have, a little. Teaching is definitely harder on me now than it used to be. Plus, it feels like the schools are making more work for us with all the testing they do and whatnot. It would be nice to have more time to do the things I'd like to do. So maybe coming to the quilt show will inspire me. And I could bring Sterling with me, too."

"Sterling?" asked Beatrice, raising her eyebrows in surprise.

"He mentioned it in passing to me when he saw me looking at a flyer. He thought he might go and take pictures to show his students. He always comes up with really fun ideas of things to share with them."

They finished with the pots and pans and chatted about other things for a while. If Elspeth's memory was slipping, it wasn't at all evident from the conversation they had. But then, sometimes memory loss seemed to work that way.

When they were done, Elspeth hurried off to her Bible study and Beatrice to hers . . . still thinking about Petunia and all the secrets that seemed to surround her.

The next morning, Beatrice was thankful that the day started off a good deal calmer than the one before. She and Wyatt had an uninterrupted breakfast in the backyard again, this time with simple bowls of cereal and toast with jam. Noo-noo was in attendance, too, of course and spent much of her time watching a box turtle make its slow and steady way from one end of the yard to the other. She sniffed it curiously once and then skittered backward as it suddenly drew its head and feet into its shell. She barked sharply a couple of times, sounding the alarm to Wyatt and Beatrice. Her expression seemed to indicate that she strongly suspected there was a small dinosaur in the yard.

Beatrice filled Wyatt in on what she'd heard the day before since they'd both been too tired after church to really rehash everything. She talked about how she wondered if Fletcher had been a bit enamored with Petunia, if Dora's argument with Petunia had really been as fierce as Elspeth described, whether Sterling had been a bit too pushy in his pursuit of Petunia's heart, and why Elspeth had had a run-in with Petunia shortly before she died.

Wyatt said, "That's a lot to think about. I'm definitely concerned about Elspeth, and am glad to hear her daughter is going to be moving to Dappled Hills. Edgenora told me what happened with her Bible study and I wondered at the time what it meant for her teaching at the school, too."

Beatrice nodded. "It will be good for her daughter to give her a hand and keep a bit of an eye on her."

The phone rang and Beatrice picked it up and sighed. "Meadow. And I have a feeling I know what she's calling about."

Wyatt hid a small smile as Beatrice attempted to tamp down her exasperation and sound cheerful and friendly. "Good morning, Meadow."

Meadow went right to the point, completely forgoing greetings. "Did you have the chance to speak with Dora last night about the quilt show changes? What did she say? Did she scrap some of her ideas?"

Beatrice gave Wyatt a wry look and nodded. As expected, Meadow had the quilt show on her brain.

"No, I didn't, as a matter of fact. I was busy talking with Sterling Wade and Elspeth. I'll try to catch up with Dora later today, Meadow."

Meadow's voice was glum on the other end of the line. "Oh. Well, it sounds like you had a lot going on last night at church. What did you find out? Did they have any ideas what might have happened to Petunia?"

"I didn't learn a whole lot, I'm afraid. Sterling Wade did seem to be infatuated by Petunia. He mentioned that Petunia and Elspeth had argued lately, but when I spoke with Elspeth, she acted as if she barely knew Petunia and hadn't really interacted with her at all."

Meadow snorted. "I bet she did act all innocent. If Elspeth had an argument with poor Petunia, do you think she'd want to admit to it? Although I think Ramsay also caught wind of some sort of quarrel between the two of them because he was asking me questions about Elspeth, himself."

"Have you heard anything else from Ramsay?"

Meadow said, "Nothing useful. Just a few absentminded grunts when I asked him questions. Oh, and he said he wants to *retire*. Can you imagine? He'll be underfoot all day with his newspapers and notebooks. He'll eat all day and leave plates and cups out. And he'll be messing with my routine."

As far as Beatrice could tell, Meadow didn't really *have* much of a routine. Or, if she did, it consisted of going with the flow.

"If he does retire, he'll probably stay well out of the way, writing short stories and poetry," said Beatrice in what she hoped was a soothing voice. And it was true: how else would Ramsay be able to write with Meadow's constant chatter, Boris-the-dog's nonsense, and the clattering of pots and pans if he didn't squirrel himself away into a remote corner of the house to concentrate?

"Maybe," said Meadow, sounding doubtful. But then she added, more cheerfully, "There is the fact that he's mentioned wanting to retire before and then doesn't. That's frequently all that becomes of it—his just *saying* he wants to."

"What's changed his mind on it before?" asked Beatrice.

"He didn't think the other potential candidates for his job would be as good as he is," said Meadow fondly. She paused. "He's probably right. He does have a way with people, and everyone in Dappled Hills trusts him. He's practically an institution in this town. Besides, he cares about the town and wants to keep things calm and peaceful here."

Beatrice glanced at her watch and said, "I'd better run, Meadow. It's my day to pick up Will from preschool and I have a few things to do before then."

"Enjoy your time with him this afternoon," said Meadow warmly. "The little love. Oh, and his favorite songs right now are Itsy-Bitsy-Spider and The Wheels on the Bus. And tell him a fairy tale from memory, like *Jack-and-the-Beanstalk*."

Beatrice hung up and sighed, looking ruefully at Wyatt. "Meadow signed off by telling me all of Will's current favorite things to sing and hear. No pressure."

Wyatt gave her a refill on her coffee and said, "Just remember, Will has a great time over here too and his visits with you don't need to be exactly like his visits with Meadow. Two grandmothers, two different fun experiences, right?"

Beatrice gave him a hug. He really did have the knack of knowing just what to say.

Beatrice spent her morning getting the cottage organized. There were quilting scraps scattered everywhere that needed to go back in her carefully sorted piles, a stack of newspapers and magazines that needed to go into the recycling bin, and some unopened mail that needed attending to. Then she took Noo-noo on a walk and the little dog trotted happily in front of her, grinning at the world until she'd find something that desperate-ly needing sniffing at the side of the road. Then she was in the mood to really trot quickly all the way back home (possibly be-cause of the promise of lunch ahead of her) and Beatrice was quite breathless by the time they arrived at her front door.

Which, of course, was when her cell phone rang. Glancing at it, she saw it was Dora and repressed a groan. She wasn't quite in the frame of mind to have a conversation with Dora yet. She definitely needed to be on her A-game when she did.

"Dora," she said, still breathlessly.

"Goodness, I must have interrupted you in the middle of something," said Dora briskly. Beatrice, as always, had the impression that Dora was likely furiously multitasking in the background. From the noises she could hear in the background, it appeared Dora was unloading her dishwasher as she spoke on the phone. Perhaps she was unloading the dishwasher, talking on the phone, and also putting a casserole together for later—Beatrice wouldn't doubt that Dora could juggle multiple tasks with ease.

"No, no, I was just coming back from a walk with my dog, that's all."

"Sounds like a rather lively walk," said Dora with a snorting laugh. "Well, I'll let you go, I just wanted to see if you could possibly meet me at the Patchwork Cottage shop in an hour. I felt we needed to check in with each other on our progress for the quilting show and see where we are."

Beatrice's mind whirled. She was under the distinct impression that she hadn't *had* any progress to make on the quilting show. Had she been given some sort of assignment? When? Dora had basically taken over the entire thing, just as she'd told Meadow. "All right," she said faintly.

"Perfect. I'll look forward to getting filled in." The sounds of dishes being put into cabinets stopped and now there was a sound very much like a vacuum cleaner being pulled out of a closet. "I'll see you then."

Beatrice hung up as the vacuum started roaring on the other end of the line. Although she had a very productive morning, it suddenly seemed like quite a meager effort in comparison to Dora's overwhelming productivity.

She fed Noo-noo, prepared and ate a quick tomato sandwich and some red grapes, and took a few, calming minutes reading her book before driving over to the quilt shop to face Dora.

The Patchwork Cottage itself was a pretty calming place for Beatrice, although possibly not with the additional presence of Dora Tucker. There was soft folk music playing over the store speakers . . . it was always a local group of musicians since Posy, the shop owner, loved to promote the work of regional artists. There were quilts everywhere: draped over vintage sewing machines, hanging on the walls and from the ceiling, and over the backs of sofas and armchairs in the store's sitting area. Everything was soft and low-key and welcoming. The shop made Beatrice feel more creative almost by osmosis. And today, Posy had put out cookies and brownies on a table near the sitting area. They must have still been warm because Beatrice could smell the sweet aroma.

Posy was checking out a customer at the register but gave Beatrice a cheery wave as she walked in. Beatrice walked toward the sitting area a bit warily before seeing that she'd actually beaten Dora to the shop. Miss Sissy, a very senior fellow quilter and neighbor of Beatrice's was already there, snoring lustily on the sofa before awaking with a start and glaring at Beatrice reproachfully, although Beatrice had been quite sure she hadn't made a sound.

Maisie, the shop cat who was jointly owned by Miss Sissy and Posy, opened her eyes sleepily, gave Beatrice a small mew in recognition, and fell right back to sleep on Miss Sissy's lap.

"Where's Will?" demanded the old woman, gazing at Beatrice through narrowed eyes as if Beatrice was simply not acceptable on her own and without the presence of the baby.

Beatrice decided it was time to practice her patience. She was going to need it with the conversation with Dora and thought it might be best to try it out on Miss Sissy. She gave Miss Sissy a beaming smile and said, "Will is at preschool this morning, remember? Piper drops him off at preschool and then I pick him up."

Beatrice interpreted Miss Sissy's responding expression to mean that she'd much rather be spending time with the baby than with Beatrice. Beatrice added, "At least you have Maisie right now to keep you company. And you can see Will later with me."

"Bah," said Miss Sissy.

Maisie, perhaps disturbed by the 'bah' or perhaps wanting to check out the Noo-noo smells on Beatrice, leapt agilely from Miss Sissy's lap into Beatrice's.

"Bah!" said Miss Sissy again, more fervently this time.

Beatrice wasn't quite sure how to respond to this, but fortunately didn't have to as Miss Sissy rose from the sofa and stomped away in the direction of the refreshments Posy had put out. Considering Miss Sissy's massive and ever-unappeased appetite, Beatrice hoped Posy had plenty of replacement cookies and brownies.

Posy came over and took Miss Sissy's spot on the sofa while the shop was quiet. "How are you?" she asked, her bright blue eyes clouded with concern. "I heard what happened at the elementary school yesterday. Is Piper all right? Was she friends with the teacher?"

Beatrice nodded, stroking Maisie as she curled up into a ball on her lap. "She wasn't exactly close to Petunia, but I think they were becoming friends. Piper had stopped by her room to say hi to her yesterday morning. She'll be all right, but it was quite a shock, of course." She glanced over at Miss Sissy, moodily eating a brownie across the room. "How is everything going here?"

Posy followed her gaze and sighed. "I think Miss Sissy is at loose ends. The mechanic decided her car was totaled, you know."

Beatrice did know. She also knew the reason the car was totaled in the first place—Miss Sissy had barreled into a house. She *had* barreled into the house on purpose. However, it was Beatrice's opinion that the town of Dappled Hills was a lot safer with Miss Sissy off the streets, no matter how temporary it might be.

Posy fretted, "Apparently, the cost of repairing the car would be a lot more than it's actually worth. So I think it's been generally decided that Miss Sissy has now been taken off the roads for good."

Beatrice's eyes grew big. "Really? No, that's excellent news, Posy. I was always worried Miss Sissy was going to be the cause of some horrific accident. How is Miss Sissy taking it?"

They both looked across the room again where Miss Sissy had launched into eating another brownie. "Well, I think she's coming around to the idea. After all, she can walk pretty much everywhere she wants to go from her house. And I give her rides to the shop in the mornings."

"She's in great shape to walk everywhere, too," said Beatrice, looking at the old woman's surprisingly strong and wiry frame. "She's strong as a horse. I have no idea how old she is, but I think she might have more strength than I do and she must be a generation older."

"Yes. But of course she misses her car. You know how Miss Sissy loved to drive around."

"Often on the sidewalks," murmured Beatrice. Again, she felt relieved that Miss Sissy's driving days had come to a close. Mr. Toad's wild ride had finally come to a stop.

Suddenly the bell on the door rang enthusiastically as it opened wide and they could hear Dora's strident voice calling out. "Hello there! Good morning to you."

Posy started to stand, but Dora waved her back down again. "No, no, just take a seat and I'll sit next to you. There's no point in standing when you don't have to—you're on your feet all day, Posy. I don't know how you do it."

Dora strode briskly over to the sofa and plopped down next to Posy. Maisie, the shop cat, gave Dora a disapproving look from Beatrice's lap, likely related to the volume of her voice or the force of the plopping.

Dora gave Posy and Beatrice a perceptive look and then said, "I've interrupted something. You two were talking about something important."

Posy lowered her voice, glancing at Miss Sissy, still moodily munching away. The refreshments were clearly going to need re-freshing. "Just about Miss Sissy. She's been at loose ends lately."

Dora wagged her finger. "This confirms something I already thought I knew. I *thought* she was looking somewhat the worse for wear when I saw her out the other day. Moody. Certainly off, at any rate."

The three of them looked over again at the old woman eating. Miss Sissy narrowed her eyes suspiciously and glared at them, chewing ferociously.

"I was thinking," here Dora lowered her voice, too, "that I needed to step in. Take action. I have a plan."

Beatrice was proud of herself for not rolling her eyes. Dora and all her various plans were exhausting. She always seemed to have one. Regardless of the fact that these plans were well-conceived and well-executed, it was tiring being around someone who was always trying to fix things. Even if they were efficiently fixed.

Posy leaned in eagerly. "What were you thinking?"

"Involvement," said Dora emphatically. "Miss Sissy needs involvement."

Posy and Beatrice looked doubtfully at each other.

Chapter Six

But Dora continued on, convinced. "She should have more of a role in the quilt show. We can pull her into set-up or take-down."

Posy's eyebrows drew together in concern. "Might she be a bit too frail to take part in those things?" She looked at Beatrice. "I mean, we were just saying how very strong she was, but being strong enough to walk all over town and being strong enough to setup or take down a quilt show is very different. How old do you think Miss Sissy is?"

Beatrice shrugged. "Eighty? Ninety? Older?"

Dora shook her head vigorously. "Age is just a number. She's strong as an ox. You can see how wiry and spry she is."

The three of them studied Miss Sissy again in an evaluating way and again were glared at.

"But I've been thinking she could become more involved than just the quilt show." Here Dora looked directly at Beatrice. "I'd like to see her at church."

Beatrice said quickly, "Miss Sissy attends church every Sunday."

"Yes, but attending church doesn't have to be *just* Sunday mornings," said Dora as if Beatrice, although the minister's wife, didn't quite grasp the slippery concept. "I was thinking she needs to belong to a group at church . . . folks who can be friends and support, too. She could broaden her circle a little bit. Find some stimulation outside of her house."

There was a growling sound from Miss Sissy's direction.

"Bible study?" offered Posy slowly.

"Choir," said Dora firmly.

"Choir?!" Beatrice and Posy echoed in disbelief. They looked at each other in horror. Beatrice couldn't imagine anything vaguely melodious coming from Miss Sissy's vocal chords.

"Why not? It meets for practice on Wednesday nights. She can come to church, have a nice meal, and then practice with the group. On Sundays, she'll just spend all morning at church for the two services. She'll have a lot more interaction. It will be perfect." Dora's voice was as satisfied as if she'd just personally enacted world peace. "I'll speak with the choir director myself. The choir consists of a wonderful, giving group of people. I think it will go extremely well."

Beatrice said, "I'm not sure Miss Sissy has the voice for choir, Dora. The choir director would really have to make that call. Beth is very particular about having the voices meld in a particular way. Besides, the only vocalization I've ever heard Miss Sissy make is sort of a barking sound. That's her usual tone of voice."

Dora tsked. "Yes, but singing is different. You can have an ugly speaking voice but a beautifully harmonious singing voice.

Think about Jim Nabors from The Andy Griffith Show. He had a very nasal drawl and a lovely baritone."

Beatrice and Posy looked doubtfully at Dora, although Dora had sounded quite convincing on this point.

"Don't worry . . . I'll be the one to bring it up with Miss Sissy. Change can be difficult, can't it? But when we *have* changed, we see how much better everything can be. Then we'll make time with Beth for an audition of sorts. I'll make sure there's no pressure on Miss Sissy. I have it all in hand."

Posy gave her a worried look as if not at all sure this was in hand. The bell rang on the shop door again and she murmured an apology as she left to help a customer.

Beatrice tried to collect her scattered thoughts, feeling Dora had just completely hijacked them. She attempted to mentally reconstruct her plan to stop Dora's changes for the quilt show: the reported rock music and the lack of a cake table.

She decided to start with the music. Beatrice cleared her throat. "Isn't the folk music Posy has playing in the shop lovely?"

Dora, still musing on 'Fixing Miss Sissy', grunted in response, not really listening.

Beatrice continued, "They're all local musicians. I think that's very nice, don't you?"

Another grunt from Dora as she took out her phone and appeared to be adding tasks on her calendar, likely all Miss Sissy related.

"I was thinking it might be nice if we borrowed some of Posy's music from the shop and used it for the quilt show," finished Beatrice quickly. "That's ordinarily what we play as background music at the show and it has a rather soothing effect."

Now she had Dora's full attention. Dora laid down her phone and narrowed her eyes at Beatrice. "I was thinking live music might be more of a draw. I'm not at all sure that 'soothing' is really the effect we're looking for at a quilt show. I strongly believe attendees need to feel renewed. Revitalized. Ready to take on the rest of their week after having a wonderful experience surrounded by the arts. They're refilling their creative wells and what better way than by enjoying art and music all at once.

Beatrice remembered Meadow's horror over the thought of anything detracting or distracting from the quilts. However, live music *could* prove a draw, especially to get folks who might not have originally have considered attending a quilt show. Then, maybe, while they were at the event, they could learn more about the art of quilting and perhaps even become interested in trying it, themselves. She cautiously replied in a noncommittal tone, "That's an interesting idea."

Beatrice had planned on expounding on that statement, but Dora interrupted her. "That's one of the changes I thought I'd speak with you about. It's important to try different and new things, isn't it? Just because things have always been a particular way doesn't mean that we can't and shouldn't change things, Beatrice. What about younger people? What about bringing in folks who might fall in love with quilting and find the hobby of their hearts? Maybe bringing in a band to liven things up might even ensure more of the husbands attend than usual. We have to keep moving forward. We have to keep thinking outside of the box."

"Actually," said Beatrice, "most of the husbands *do* attend and not only to support their wives. We have a good number of husbands who do some quilting, themselves. My son-in-law is one of them. And, of course, the shows are known for delicious food, too, which helps with attendance. June Bug's cakes are always in high demand and a lot of people who regularly attend look forward to them as a highlight of the event."

Dora automatically nodded as if listening intently to Beatrice's every word, but her mind was apparently sprinting forward ahead of Beatrice's. "Right. I was thinking we could play around with that aspect of the show, too. In terms of the foods offered, I mean. Try something different . . . maybe something a little more filling."

"More filling than cake?" Beatrice heard her voice pitch into the realm of incredulity and reminded herself to bring it down a notch when she next spoke.

"I was thinking we could have sandwiches for sale, along with individual bags of chips. You know, something *different*. I'd like for the folks attending to think of the quilt show as an entire package: they can get a light meal. They can enjoy live entertainment. They can experience beautiful art."

"That's different, all right," said Beatrice levelly.

She waited for Dora to ask her what she thought of her proposed changes, but there was no question forthcoming. Tamping down her irritation, she said, "The thing is, Dora, I don't really see why we should mess with success. It will mean a lot more work to bring in live music: we need to set up for that, clear a space. We'll need to find, audition, and pay the musicians. And the quilt show is mere days away. It all seems very last-minute."

Dora was already shaking her head. "We won't have to do any of those things. My nephew's band is happy to play for free for the pleasure of playing and the experience of a larger audience than they might ordinarily play for. They're able to set up the space, themselves. People will be allowed to tip them if they want."

Beatrice continued, "All right, but there's still the fact that it's not what people *expect*. This particular quilt show has been an annual tradition since long before I moved to Dappled Hills. Families attend each year and they have certain elements that they look forward to."

Dora narrowed her eyes. "I don't really think that's as big of a deal as you think. People like surprises."

"Do they?" asked Beatrice. "I know I have a hard time adjusting to change. And I don't particularly enjoy being surprised."

Dora looked at Beatrice as if she was a very odd specimen of a human being. "Just the same, I think we should give it a go. It could be a major success."

"To be clear, what *type* of music does your nephew's band play?"

Dora shrugged a shoulder. "You know—popular music. Music that makes people want to move, dance."

"Rock music?" asked Beatrice delicately.

"I suppose that's what you'd call it. It's lively, at any rate."

Beatrice said, "I'm just not sure that's going to be a good *fit* for our attendees." She thought of Meadow, who'd been practically apoplectic over the plan. "We frequently have a lot of seniors who attend and I don't think they'd want anything very loud playing. Loud music makes it difficult to engage with others and have conversations. Visiting with others and interacting with quilters has always been an important part of the shows."

"This would give us the opportunity to appeal to a broader demographic," said Dora stubbornly. "And I could make sure they keep their volume down. I'm not a fan of loud music, myself. In fact, I had trouble with it just recently when a neighbor was playing music too loudly at all hours of the night."

Beatrice shook her head. "Even so, I just don't see it working." She paused. "If we do decide to go with live music, can your nephew's group play music *other* than rock music?"

Dora tilted her head to one side. "Such as?"

"Well, could they play jazz? Folk music? New age? Beach music? Something a little softer?"

Dora considered this. "That might work. I do think they're a band of very talented youngsters. They might like the opportunity to try something new, themselves. I'll inquire." Then, just as if she was following the points of a set mental agenda, she added, "There was another item I wanted to speak with you about. Poor Petunia's death."

At the mention of Petunia, Dora pulled out a ready handkerchief and swabbed her eyes. "Sorry," she said briskly. "I don't seem to have quite gotten over my emotional response to her death."

"Nor should you. The two of you were friends, I believe? Wyatt mentioned you'd been kind enough to introduce Petunia around church and to help her get involved."

"We were also neighbors." Dora gave a short laugh. "As a matter of fact, she was responsible for the loud music I just mentioned. But we got that worked out. I can't believe she's gone.

So young and with her whole life ahead of her. Such a terrible thing."

"It must have been quite a shock for you," said Beatrice.

"It was. I was just waking up for the day, actually. I'm more of a night owl than a morning lark and I get a lot of work done late at night. I woke to lots of text messages from women at the church about Petunia and I simply couldn't believe it. I'd just seen her the afternoon before. I thought they must have been mistaken—and for her to die in such a way?" Dora shook her head and then blew her nose forcefully.

Beatrice waited until Dora continued, "She was like a little sister to me. Petunia seemed eager to get involved with the community and I was trying to help her find her niche with different groups at the church. I was so delighted when she moved in next door. It was like a breath of fresh air in the neighborhood to have someone so young and vital moving in."

"I hate to admit it, but I really didn't even spend enough time with Petunia to really form an impression of her. What was she like?"

Dora considered this carefully. "She seemed very conscientious about the school and the kids. And she was cautious about her involvement with the church because she said she always gave everything one-hundred percent so she wanted to make sure she didn't take on too much. She was friendly and outgoing." She paused. "But she could honestly also be very opinionated. She had lots of *ideas* about *improvements* to common procedures at church."

Beatrice bit her tongue before she could say that all sounded very familiar. She didn't think Dora would appreciate the observation.

"I'm sure that coming from another town, she might have seen other approaches that worked well," said Beatrice mildly. "Sometimes it's good to have a fresh perspective."

Dora said huffily, "I'm not sure anything at the church needs improving at all. It's one thing to improve a quilt show and quite another to find things lacking with the house of God."

"I'm sure Petunia was probably only looking for ways to make things even better."

Dora said, "But it sort of implies criticism, doesn't it? I thought it did."

Perhaps only to people who were a bit too fiercely protective, figured Beatrice.

"But all in all, Petunia was a lovely person. Warm and caring and eager to engage with people," said Dora. "She sounded like she was a fantastic schoolteacher and she was interested in being a Sunday school teacher at the church. There were so many things she was looking forward to doing, so much that she had to give. I simply couldn't believe it when I heard the news. What's the world coming to? And a murder in a school?"

"I'm sure Ramsay will get to the bottom of it soon," said Beatrice. "He and the state police seem to be all over it."

Miss Sissy stomped back in their direction, and Posy, who'd just finished ringing up the quilter's purchase, joined them, too. Posy glanced over in the direction of her snacks table and blinked a bit when she saw the snacks were completely annihilated.

Dora sat a little straighter and said cheerfully, "Miss Sissy! Just the lady I wanted to see."

Miss Sissy narrowed her eyes at her suspiciously.

"I was thinking it would be marvelous to have you more involved with church. I really think you can make such a positive impact there," said Dora.

The wizened old woman scowled at her. "I go to church."

"Yes, and you're very regular, too," said Dora as if she kept a personal attendance log. Which, knowing Dora, could perhaps be true. "But I was thinking you could become even *more* involved."

Posy started looking a bit concerned as if Dora would set her sights on her next and she didn't have a lot of extra time.

Miss Sissy grunted, but seemed receptive to hearing more.

"How about if you were to join the *choir*?" asked Dora in a persuasive tone.

Posy's eyes widened.

Miss Sissy's eyes did, too. Then they narrowed again.

Dora continued blithely on, confident in the appeal of the idea. "We can use another voice in our group. Sometimes, when we don't have full attendance in choir, we sound a little weak."

Miss Sissy looked at Posy, then at Beatrice. Posy seemed at a loss for words. Beatrice offered, "Do you *like* to sing, Miss Sissy? Does this sound like something that could be interesting?"

Miss Sissy considered this. "Don't really sing," she said gruffly.

"And why would you?" asked Dora. "I live alone and I don't sing by myself unless I have music playing. I do have music that my nephew's band recorded and sometimes I find myself singing along to that. But otherwise, why would someone living alone sing?"

Beatrice pressed her lips together. Dora was really pushing the nephew and his rotten band. And she didn't want to think Dora was pushing Miss Sissy into joining choir. In fact, the whole idea irritated her much more than the quilt show changes did. She quickly said, "You certainly don't have to make a decision about that now, Miss Sissy. And it's not something you have to do at all, if you don't want to."

Dora glared at Beatrice and Beatrice lifted her chin and stared coolly at her. Finally, Dora dropped her gaze and said gruffly, "Of course you don't, Miss Sissy. I just thought it might be something you'd enjoy and a good outlet for you. I could pick you up and drive you there since I'm there on Wednesday nights for practice, anyway."

Miss Sissy growled at her, "Don't need a ride. Live right down from the church."

Dora looked annoyed, as if nothing was really going as planned with this conversation. "Whatever you want to do . . . you're the boss. Just let me know if you'd like to meet with Beth, the choir director and I can set that up." She looked at her watch. "Mercy. I need to be getting along. I have another meeting in five minutes. Good to see you all." And with that, she bustled out the door.

Beatrice relaxed a bit as she left. Dora felt like a force of nature and not one of the good ones: more like a hurricane or a tornado. She turned to Miss Sissy, who was looking mulish. "What do you think of all that, Miss Sissy?"

Miss Sissy levelled a stare at her. "Brownies and cookies are gone."

Posy quickly leapt into action as if relieved to be doing something else. "I'll get more."

Beatrice had the feeling Miss Sissy didn't really want to discuss getting more involved. In fact, the old woman seemed to prefer it when she made decisions completely on her own.

This was confirmed when Miss Sissy said, "Let's go get Will."

It didn't surprise Beatrice in the slightest that Miss Sissy had memorized when Will was out of preschool (although the old woman frequently seemed to forget which days Beatrice had Will and which ones Meadow did).

"I think we'll get there a bit too early if we go now. Maybe ten more minutes? Otherwise, we'll cut short his show-and-tell time." Although Beatrice did love to sometimes go early and watch show-and-tell. The classroom had a two-way mirror window and so parents and caregivers could watch unobserved by the kids. Will brought the same toy every day for this baby version of show-and-tell . . . his current favorite lovey, a stuffed giraffe. She loved seeing his expression as the little boy pulled it out of his tiny backpack to show the class: proud and happy to be snuggling with his toy again.

The bell on the door rang violently and Meadow's face appeared in the doorway. She glanced around the shop frantically until she spotted Beatrice. Then, just as suddenly, her face disappeared. Then reappeared. "Sorry," she said breathless and flushed. "I'm walking Boris."

And Boris, apparently, was intrigued by something farther down the sidewalk past the quilt shop. It seemed more as if Boris, actually, was walking Meadow than the other way around.

"Boris!" hissed Meadow. She rolled her eyes. "It's Mrs. Sparrow's little cocker spaniel. Boris is fascinated by her. I swear he wants to have her for his sweetheart." She reined her focus in on Beatrice. "Did you talk to Dora?"

Beatrice nodded.

"Well, how did it go?" asked Meadow impatiently as she engaged in an invisible tug of war she seemed to be losing on the other side of the door.

"Not so well," admitted Beatrice. "Dora is excellent at getting her own way."

"Did you bring up all of our concerns?" asked Meadow frantically. "The rock music and the nephew? The cakes she was trying to eliminate? The changes that no one will like that will drive away our regulars from all future quilt shows? The fact that this is all very last-minute? The disaster that will ensue?" Meadow sounded very much like she might be referring to a pending apocalypse than a quilting event.

"Yes. And the only concession I got was that the band might play something other than rock music. Under the circumstances and considering who I was dealing with, I thought I came out rather well."

Posy's eyes were wide. "Oh my," she said with a chuckle.

Meadow, yanked forward by Boris and then yanked back, said indignantly, "This can't be the end of it. I'll speak with Dora too and voice my worry about the changes."

"Dora seems to think these adjustments will help bring in a new group of attendees. That we might be able to appeal to a different demographic and encourage newbies to give quilting a try. Dora believes change is good," said Beatrice mildly.

"How could she say such a thing when it so *rarely* is!" Meadow was fuming now. Then, abruptly, she disappeared completely from the door. They spotted her in front of the shop window, giving them a shrug as she allowed Boris to spirit her away somewhere far down the sidewalk after the alluring cocker spaniel.

Chapter Seven

Beatrice glanced at her watch and turned to Miss Sissy, who was still frowning at the door where Meadow's visage had last been seen as if waiting for it to pop back like an overwrought Jack-in-the-box. "Ready to head out? I think we'll get to the preschool at the perfect time. Maybe we can see a little of his show-and-tell before we take him home."

Miss Sissy was already bustling for the door by the end of her sentence.

Beatrice drove over to the church preschool and parked the car. Miss Sissy was striding ahead of her again as they headed for the covered preschool entrance around the back of the church. As expected, they were able to watch Will's class do a babyish version of show-and-tell. They packed, or their moms did, one favorite thing in their backpacks from home and then sat on the show-and-tell chair with help when it was their turn and showed it to the class as the preschool teacher narrated and the child beamed proudly, each little one around ten months to a year old. Miss Sissy and Beatrice saw dolls, stuffed animals, blankets, and other loveys being happily presented. Will, as Beatrice had figured, had brought his giraffe and ended the short presentation by burying his small face in the stuffed animal.

Then the little ones (mostly . . . there were a few stragglers) gathered in a loose circle, swayed back and forth as the teacher sang a goodbye song, collected their diminutive backpacks, and eagerly waited for their parents.

Miss Sissy and Beatrice, first on the scene, stuck their heads in the door to get Will. Miss Sissy beamed as the little boy toddled over and gave her a hug after giving Beatrice one. Beatrice took one hand and Miss Sissy his other and they walked very slowly to the parking lot, Will humming the whole way.

When they got back to Beatrice's cottage, Miss Sissy asked, "Stroller ride?"

Beatrice shook her head. "No, I don't think so, Miss Sissy. Usually Will is ready for his afternoon nap as soon as he gets back from school. Preschool wears him out and they have lunch right before show-and-tell, and that makes him sleepy, too."

Judging from Miss Sissy's stormy expression, this alternate plan didn't sit well with her.

Beatrice suggested, "We could take naps, too. There's the hammock outside and the temperature today would be great for sleeping in it. The sofa is pretty comfortable, too. Afternoon naps are wonderful, you know. We'll wake up all refreshed and ready to take on the rest of our day."

Miss Sissy, although ordinarily a nap aficionado, knit her brows ferociously.

Beatrice sighed. "All right. Maybe a short stroller ride. But you'll have to help me keep Will awake and engaged. If he falls asleep even for a few minutes during the stroller ride, it'll totally mess his nap schedule up and Piper will have a wild Will on her hands when she picks him up."

Miss Sissy was already pulling the stroller out. And Will, who loved stroller rides, was toddling behind her with interest. He clutched his giraffe to make sure the toy came with him.

Noo-noo gave Beatrice a forlorn expression and she stooped to rub her. "Sorry, girl," she said softly. "I'll take you next time. I think there's too much to wrangle for this walk."

Beatrice felt a bit unsettled by going on the unscheduled walk, which was also very much the feeling she'd gotten earlier when she'd spoken with Dora. At the very least, she figured she could control the direction of the stroller ride. "Let's go this way," she said, nodding in the direction of Meadow's house. She had no intention of seeing Meadow again, but thought there might be more to see in that direction. And more to keep Will stimulated . . . and, all-importantly, awake.

Fortunately, Miss Sissy didn't seem to care a whit which direction they set off in. So she took Beatrice's suggestion. They also passed Miss Sissy's house along the way, which caused the old woman to stop the stroller, stoop down, and point it out to the little boy. Will gaped at the house, as well he might—the small house, completely engulfed in vines, had always reminded Beatrice of the castle in Sleeping Beauty that was eaten up by thorny vegetation.

They moved on and soon approached another cottage, this one with a very tidy yard that was being tidied even more by a woman with long brown curls and glasses. Beatrice looked closer and realized it was Edie King, Fletcher's wife. Edie spotted them and waved before coming over to coo at Will, who smiled sleepily back at her.

"So this is your little grandbaby," said Edie, crouching down to Will's level. He shyly held out his stuffed giraffe to her and she added, "Is this your giraffe? He's so sweet!" She handed the stuffed animal back to him and then stood up again. "And the *baby's* sweet, too. I've heard so much about him from Wyatt."

"We think he's sweet, too," said Beatrice, eyes twinkling. "How are you doing, Edie? Are you and Fletcher settling in well here? I'm sorry I haven't been by—I'm a very poor excuse for a neighbor."

Edie looked wryly at Will. "Well, I think you probably have your hands full. Don't worry about it."

Beatrice said, "And I wanted to tell you how much I enjoyed the music during the service a couple of Sundays ago. I think you were the acting music director that day?"

She smiled at Beatrice. "Thank you! Yes, Jenny was out that day, so I stepped in for her."

Beatrice said, "Wyatt has mentioned several times how lucky we are to have you. He said you play quite a few instruments?"

"That's right." Edie paused, looking at Will. "He's fallen asleep. Must have been a long day."

"Oh, goodness!" Beatrice stooped down and rubbed Will's arm. "He doesn't need to sleep until he's back in his bed or it will mess his nap up later." She glanced over at Miss Sissy as if to tell her told-you-so, but the old woman not only looked completely unconcerned, she also looked rather bored by the conversation.

Edie gestured toward the house. "Fletcher and I have a tank full of tropical fish. Do you think he'd like to see them? They might keep him from nodding off again. There are a ton of different kinds and they're all very colorful."

Beatrice gave her a grateful look. "That would be great, yes. I know Piper and Ash *only* frequent restaurants with fish tanks inside and gravel parking lots outside. Both things keep Will entertained while they're waiting to be seated or for their meals to come."

The fish tank was large and indeed impressive. Edie turned on a light and the whole rectangular tank glowed, light glinting off the colorful gills of the fish. Will thankfully looked mesmerized and not a bit sleepy now, eyes alert as he watched them swim and pointed a chubby finger to show Miss Sissy a particularly pretty fish.

"Whew," said Beatrice to Edie. "That was a close one. Not only did I not want to mess up Will's nap for my sake, Piper would have been none too pleased, either because he'd have been cranky the rest of the day until his bedtime. Now he'll be the perfect angel he usually is instead of turning into a little bear."

Miss Sissy seemed just as mesmerized by the fish as Will was. She pulled up a chair and picked up Will from the stroller and clutched him on her lap while they watched them swim around, the fishes' bright colors swirling around each other, tails swishing.

Edie gave Beatrice a sympathetic look. "You've had a busy week so far, haven't you? I know you've been at the church a lot.

The quilt show is coming up, I know. And now you have your grandbaby." She mouthed, "And Miss Sissy."

Beatrice said, "It's been busy, but I have to say it's better than being bored. When things get too quiet, I start getting restless." She gave a rueful smile. "When I was working over forty hours a week, all I could think about was how great retirement was going to be. I pictured myself in a hammock all day long with a stack of books and a lemonade next to me. I thought I'd read in between napping."

"It hasn't been that way?" asked Edie. "Because I sort of have the same retirement fantasy."

"Oh, it's nice. And I do lie in the hammock and I do have a stack of books to read from the library as well as a bunch on my Kindle I need to read. But the funny thing is that my body apparently doesn't know what to *do* with the fact that I'm not working. So I'll lie in the hammock and suddenly get up to empty the dishwasher or make a phone call or mop the kitchen floor. So now I'm kind of reeling back my expectations for retirement to something a little easier to attain—like reading for an hour and *then* jumping up to do thirty minutes of yardwork or walk the dog or whatever. Staying busy does help."

Edie nodded. "I know what you mean. If I'm not busy, my days crawl by. That's one reason I'm selling real estate *and* helping out at the church. Real estate can be feast or famine so I like to have something else I can work on in case things are slow at the office. There were so many weddings last summer that Jenny and I had to divide them up."

"That must be a little stressful, right?" asked Beatrice. "I hear that brides can be pretty demanding."

Edie smiled in remembrance. "Believe it or not, I loved every minute of it. I loved playing different songs for the brides to decide on, orchestrating the music and the soloist. It was so much fun for me. But I'll look forward to slowing down a little. I've been trying to make a little extra money to pad our savings account a little. Fletcher and I would love to start a family, but we'd like a nest egg before we do."

Beatrice said, "Oh, that's wonderful! Maybe your baby and Will can play together sometimes."

They chatted about odds and ends for a few minutes before Edie turned somber. "I heard about yesterday from Fletcher, of course. We were both so shocked over it and I'm sure Piper was, too."

"It's horrible, isn't it? I felt terrible for poor Petunia. I really only knew her through Piper, which is a pity because I know she was getting involved at the church. Did you know her from there?" asked Beatrice.

"Not very well. I'd met her a couple of times at church but didn't really get to know her. When I did meet her, she seemed like a lovely person and a wonderful addition to the community. Everything I heard about Petunia was positive: she was a great teacher, a good volunteer. It's all such a shame. I know Fletcher knew her fairly well—he was really shaken up."

Beatrice said, "That must have been a real shock for him, finding Petunia that way."

Edie gave Beatrice a blank look, which she quickly covered up. She hastily said, "It must have been."

Beatrice had the distinct impression Edie hadn't been aware that Fletcher had found Petunia. Had he not wanted his wife to know that he'd sought out Petunia before school?

Beatrice said, "I had to go pick Piper up at school when it happened because she was so shaken up. Did you have to do the same with Fletcher or was he able to get home all right afterward?"

"He actually didn't call me at all. I think he was so upset that he didn't even think to call. I'd been at home, getting ready for my day and jumped when I heard him coming through the front door. I about jumped through my skin." Edie switched her attention from Beatrice to Will and Miss Sissy, still watching the fish.

Beatrice had the feeling Edie might be prevaricating, somehow. There was something about her that made her feel Edie wasn't completely telling the truth. She couldn't quite put her finger on it.

"I can't imagine who could do such a thing, can you?" asked Beatrice. "As you mentioned, everyone has such positive things to say about Petunia. And she hadn't even been living in Dappled Hills very long."

"Well, of course, everyone *does* have positive things to say after someone has died." Edie put her hand over her mouth. "Excuse that. It does tend to be true, but I shouldn't have said it. It sounds insensitive."

"Did you hear of anyone who had a problem with her?" asked Beatrice, tilting her head to one side.

"Not a problem, per se." Edie sighed. "I'm really not expressing myself very well today. What I mean to say is that I do know there was someone who was a little *too* interested in Petunia. Piper might even have told you about it . . . Fletcher told me. Sterling Wade, another teacher at the school, was apparently totally obsessed with Petunia. Fletcher thought his behavior was very unprofessional."

"Did Fletcher say he mentioned it to the police?"

Edie shook her head. "He felt uncomfortable mentioning it because he's a colleague of Sterling's and still has to work with him. But he felt Sterling was on the point of being harassing to Petunia." She made a face and lowered her voice. "You don't think he became so frustrated with his lack of progress with Petunia romantically that he could have done away with her?"

"I don't know. I suppose all possibilities are on the table in a situation like this."

Beatrice looked back over at Will. The gentle movements of the colorful fish continued to enthrall the toddler, but he was starting to get that sleepy expression again. So, in fact, was Miss Sissy. Apparently, the fish were having quite the soothing effect.

"We should probably head on back home. I know we didn't get very far on our walk, but Will needs a dedicated nap and now I think Miss Sissy does, too."

Edie smiled at the two of them, the little boy in Miss Sissy's lap. "Well, maybe you can continue your stroller ride after everyone has had some rest. Feel free to come back anytime and see the fish. I swear they were preening in their tank at all the attention."

Edie walked them outside and watched as Beatrice helped Will back into his stroller. Then she made a face as she looked around the yard. "We've got some work to do here."

Beatrice glanced around and chuckled. "Do you? I was about to say that I thought your yard looked so much better than when Nancy Roberts owned the house. You've clearly *done* a lot of work."

Edie smiled at her. "Thanks. I guess sometimes it's hard for me to pat myself on the back when I see there's still a lot to do. Fletcher has helped some, too . . . mostly on trying to fix the fence so we don't have to buy a new one." She gestured to a shovel and a few tools out in the yard and sighed. "I assume he's getting back to it at some point."

"Well, it all looks marvelous, inside and out. And you haven't even lived here very long. A couple of months?" asked Beatrice.

Edie nodded and Beatrice smiled ruefully. "I'll confess I still have a few boxes in my attic that I haven't unpacked yet, so you've more unpacked than I am, from what I can see."

They waved goodbye . . . at least, Beatrice and Will did (Will very enthusiastically, showing off his new bye-bye skills). Miss Sissy gave a big harrumph as she stomped behind the stroller.

When they got back to Beatrice's cottage, Will was starting to nod off again, but this time Beatrice wasn't worried about it. She lifted him gently from the stroller and settled him in the blue and white pack-and-play crib Ash had set up in their spare room. Miss Sissy gave the little boy his stuffed giraffe and he fell right to sleep with a happy, snuffling sigh.

Then Miss Sissy headed straight for the hammock, once again displaying her surprising agility as she leapt in, soon snoring with gusto.

Beatrice settled on the sofa so she could hear Will. She wasn't sure she needed or even wanted a nap, but after reading her book for fifteen minutes, she was off in the Land of Nod, herself.

Sometime later, Beatrice woke with the sound of Will singing happily to himself in the crib. She groggily glanced at her watch and was surprised to see she'd been asleep for over an hour. She stood up and peered out the back door to see Miss Sissy still asleep in the hammock. And Noo-noo was lying on her back on the living room floor, always a comical sight with her little corgi legs in the air and her large ears splayed on the floor, snoring just as enthusiastically as Miss Sissy had been earlier.

Beatrice collected Will, changed him, and set about getting him a snack of graham crackers and juice. Miss Sissy, who seemed to have an unerring internal radar about food being served, immediately showed up at the table, too, rubbing her eyes to banish her sleepiness. Beatrice pulled out a jar of peanut butter and she and Miss Sissy had their graham crackers with a small upgrade.

There was a tap at the door and Will swung his head in that direction. "Mama!" he cooed as Piper grinned in through the front door at him.

Beatrice let her in and gave her a hug.

"How was he?" asked Piper.

"He was a perfect angel," said Beatrice. "We went on a walk and saw Edie King's fish tank. Then he took a long nap. He's been changed and he's just finishing his snack."

Piper quirked an eyebrow. "Edie King's house, hm?"

Beatrice smiled at her. "I promise that was completely accidental . . . I wasn't even trying to be nosy or find out any information about Fletcher. I realized, also, I've not been a very friendly neighbor since I hadn't welcomed them after they moved to the street. Edie came over to talk to the baby and then Will started falling asleep when we were talking. She proposed he see her fish to keep him awake for a little while longer. Her house looked wonderful—I told her it was a vast improvement from when the previous owner was there."

"That was sweet of her. I don't even know how she had the time to move in and get everything organized. I saw that her yard looks amazing, too. So she's selling real estate, serves as the assistant choir director at the church, and somehow found the time to make sure her new house and yard look great. Oh, and she keeps Fletcher on track, too. I saw her over at the school yesterday when we were leaving."

"At the school?" Beatrice frowned. "That's funny. She said she hadn't had to pick up Fletcher from school—that he'd surprised her by coming home early."

Piper shrugged. "I don't know—it was definitely her, though. Maybe she just pulled in to see what was going on when she drove by and saw all the emergency vehicles."

Which still didn't explain why Edie had said she was at home when she found out about Petunia, though.

Miss Sissy was still focused on the peanut butter and Will was now playing with his giraffe, so Beatrice asked in a low voice, "How were things at the school today? Still a little different there?"

"It was okay. Not *completely* back to normal because there were a couple of officers there, mostly talking to the principal. The police seemed to hope we had security cameras in the halls and classrooms."

"But you don't?" asked Beatrice.

Piper shook her head. "It's an elementary school. I think the high school here has them, but we don't. We're more concerned about securing the doors once school has started. So we don't really have any idea what happened or who was responsible."

Will reached out his arms to Piper and she gently lifted him out of his high chair. Beatrice took a look at Will's hands and said, "Let me grab some damp paper towels."

She carefully cleaned him up before he could transfer graham cracker sludge to Piper's work clothes and then the little boy gave his mother a big snuggle.

"I'd better head out and get some things done around the house. Thanks so much for watching him, Mama. And Miss Sissy, thanks to you, too."

Miss Sissy grunted in acknowledgement and took a big gulp of milk to wash the peanut butter down.

After Piper and Will had left, Beatrice said brightly to Miss Sissy, "Well, now! Thanks for helping me with the baby; that was fun. Are you about ready to head out, too?"

Miss Sissy apparently wasn't. She continued sitting at the table looking mulish. Finally, she said, "Didn't get a real walk."

Beatrice stifled a sigh. "Didn't we? We walked down the street. We just took a little detour. You seemed to enjoy Edie's fish, yourself."

Miss Sissy pressed her lips together in displeasure.

"Okay. How about if you and I walk Noo-noo? I'm sure she would like to get out for a while to stretch her legs and sniff around a little and she seemed disappointed earlier when she didn't get to go with us. I didn't want to take her earlier because it was too much to juggle both a dog and the stroller."

This appeared to appease Miss Sissy, who headed straight for the door.

Beatrice stuck to the original plan for the walk since there was usually less traffic and more things for Noo-noo to explore along the way. And, as expected, Noo-noo found lots to sniff at. They even surprised a couple of does who stared solemnly at them before dashing back into the woods before Noo-noo even had the chance to bark.

Beatrice and Miss Sissy slowly made their way until they were again right in front of Edie King's house. Beatrice was lost in her thoughts next to the silent Miss Sissy until Noo-noo pulled at the leash, trying to drag Beatrice into Edie's yard. This behavior was definitely unusual. Ordinarily, Noo-noo was very good on the leash and didn't pull unless a sassy squirrel made her lose her mind for a few moments. But there was no squirrel in sight. Nor were there any bunnies or more deer, which could also prove major distractions. Beatrice frowned. "What's wrong, girl?"

Noo-noo started whining and looked up at Beatrice meaningfully.

"What is it, girl?" asked Beatrice. "Do you need water or something?"

Miss Sissy suddenly made a sort of groaning sound and clutched wildly at Beatrice's arm.

Beatrice now really *was* alarmed with both the corgi and the old woman acting out of the ordinary.

"Look!" said Miss Sissy urgently, pointing a trembling and arthritic hand toward Edie's house.

There Beatrice saw the crumpled figure of a woman at the side of the house.

Chapter Eight

It took Beatrice precisely three seconds to call Ramsay with shaking fingers after checking on Edie. Although she'd really known at once that Edie was dead from her lifeless eyes staring at her, she'd carefully tried to find a non-existent pulse. The few minutes it took Ramsay to arrive somehow felt like hours.

Beatrice and Miss Sissy stayed back on the sidewalk with the dog while Ramsay, soon joined by the state police still there in the town to investigate, blocked off the Kings' yard and started making notes and taking photos. Miss Sissy was making all sorts of noises as they did . . . grunting and mumbling to herself.

Beatrice gave her a concerned look. "Miss Sissy, do you want to go home? It's just right down the street and I'm sure Ramsay can speak with you there just as easily as he can here."

Her answer to this was a glare.

"We could sit on the curb," suggested Beatrice. "It might be better to get off your feet."

Miss Sissy was apparently not impressed with this suggestion. So they stood for another little while. Unsurprisingly, Meadow soon exploded from her house and headed with great determination in their direction, heralded to the trouble by the sirens, lights, or perhaps some sort of sixth sense.

Ramsay had just reached Miss Sissy and Beatrice with his notebook in hand when he spotted Meadow, too.

Ramsay groaned when he saw his wife approaching and swabbed his forehead with his hand. "Here we go."

He held up his hand to slow Meadow's progress before she came all the way up to them. "Meadow, just hold on a few minutes, okay? I need to speak with these ladies and hear what happened."

Meadow put her hand on her hips. "Considering I'm going to get them to tell *me* exactly what happened, we'll save time if I can listen in."

Ramsay rolled his eyes. "All right, love. But you need to keep quiet." He made tamping motions with his hands to indicate Meadow needed to take it down a notch.

Meadow pantomimed zipping her lips. Her eyes were full of concern.

Ramsay took a deep breath and then gave Beatrice and Miss Sissy a regretful smile. "Seems like you had more than you bargained for during your stroll. Think you can tell me what happened?"

Beatrice shook her head. "Honestly, we don't know very much."

"Wanted to walk," barked Miss Sissy.

Beatrice said, "Yes, Miss Sissy decided a walk was in order and Noo-noo hadn't had one so we decided to take her along. We ended up setting out and when we got up to the Kings' property, Noo-noo starting whining and pulling at her leash.

I thought maybe she needed some water, but clearly she was aware something was wrong."

They all looked down at the little dog, who stared solemnly back up at them.

"Then Miss Sissy noticed Edie King crumpled in the yard. I ran up to check for a pulse. Then I called you," finished Beatrice simply.

Meadow, who'd been doing an excellent job not saying anything, made a clucking sound and seemed agitated. Ramsay looked at her with the kind of expression you might give a bomb about to explode.

He cleared his throat. "I see. All right. And, since you're neighbors, could you help me in narrowing down the time of her death? When was the last time you saw Edie King alive?"

Miss Sissy growled, "Fish!"

Beatrice put an arm around the old woman, who was beginning to look as agitated as Meadow. "Yes, we saw her right around one o'clock. Miss Sissy and I took Will on a stroller ride after we picked him up from preschool and Edie was out working in her yard."

"What was she doing in the yard?" asked Ramsay. "Anything to do with the fence?"

Beatrice shook her head. "No, but she said Fletcher had been working on the fence earlier."

"Weeding," said Miss Sissy.

"Yes, I think she was weeding," agreed Beatrice. "Then she came down to speak with us and to see the baby. Will was nodding off while we were talking and I wanted to keep him awake so we wouldn't mess up his naptime, so she invited us inside to see her tropical fish."

"How was her state of mind?" asked Ramsay. "Did she seem anxious, upset, like something was on her mind?"

Beatrice shook her head. "Not at all. She seemed relaxed. Happy in her new house. Enjoying her gardening." She swallowed hard and said gruffly, "And looking forward to her future with Fletcher. She talked about them having a child further down the line."

Ramsay said, "Did she speak about Petunia at all? Mention her death or anything about Fletcher?"

Miss Sissy grumbled under her breath. She may not have realized they'd had that conversation since she'd been so completely mesmerized by the fish at that point.

"She did, just a little bit. Edie had nice things to say about Petunia, although she said she didn't really know her well. She mentioned Sterling Wade being very attracted to Petunia and passed along what Fletcher had thought about that . . . that it wasn't very professional. That was basically it." Then Beatrice remembered something else. "There was one thing that was odd, Ramsay. Piper mentioned to me that she'd seen Edie at the school yesterday when I was there picking her up. She figured she'd been there to collect Fletcher and take him home, but Edie told me that she hadn't known about Petunia's death until Fletcher had surprised her when he'd arrived back home."

Ramsay furrowed his brows. "So Edie was on the scene."

"According to Piper. But why would she have said she wasn't?"

He looked grim and Beatrice said, "You think she might have been there to kill Petunia. But if she'd had something to do with Petunia's death, why was she murdered? Revenge?"

Meadow made a clucking sound.

Ramsay said, "I just don't know. That's something we'll have to figure out as the investigation continues. He made some more notes. "All right, well, if I think of anything else to ask, I'll get in touch." He looked toward the road. "Oh no."

Beatrice turned and saw a white truck heading for the house. Behind the wheel, she saw Fletcher.

"We were going to send an officer to the school to speak with him," said Ramsay grimly. He looked at his watch. "Can't believe school is already out for the day."

He looked at Beatrice. "Since you're a neighbor, can you invite him over to your house to wait while the team is finished here? Do you mind?"

She shook her head and Ramsay nodded, squaring his shoulders to give Fletcher the news.

Meadow frowned. "He could come to our house. It's closer."

Beatrice shrugged. "Maybe Ramsay didn't think that was a good thing for him to offer, professionally. He's the police chief, after all. And Fletcher is a suspect."

Meadow's eyes were wide as she turned toward Fletcher. "Do you really think so?" She gazed doubtfully over at Fletcher with his square jawline and omnipresent baseball cap.

"Isn't the spouse always the primary suspect when there's a murder?" asked Beatrice. She hesitated. "I feel terrible hanging around like this but Ramsay did ask if Fletcher could come to my house. I'm starting to wonder if I should ask Wyatt to be there too, to maybe try and offer some comfort and encouragement." She took out her phone and texted him, leaving out the reason but asking if he was free. Unfortunately, he was in the middle of hospital visits the next town over. Wyatt asked if she needed him to leave, but she had the feeling by the time he got back home that Fletcher might already be gone so she told him it was fine and she'd see him later.

Fletcher was slowly getting out of the truck, his face pasty-looking as if he somehow already knew. Ramsay spoke to him and Fletcher slumped against the vehicle for support.

Miss Sissy stared at Fletcher, eyes narrowed. "Bad man."

Beatrice looked at her. "Fletcher King is? You know him?"

Miss Sissy shook her head and growled, "Don't know him. Heard him yell at Edie yesterday. After he came back home from school."

"Did you? What were they arguing about?" Meadow looked horrified.

Miss Sissy shook her head again impatiently. "*She* wasn't arguing. *He* was."

"Okay," said Beatrice absently as she watched Ramsay gesture to them. Fletcher walked slowly in their direction. "Well, I think he's about to end up with us back at my house, so try to put a lid on it, Miss Sissy. He's clearly having a rough time of it right now."

"Arguing," repeated Miss Sissy stubbornly.

"Yes, but now maybe he feels really guilty about that," said Meadow. "Just think—one of the last times he may have seen Edie, Fletcher could have exchanged hard words with her. He never got the chance to tell her how much he cared about her."

She put her hand to her chest and looked at Ramsay as if about to run over and give him a hug.

Fortunately, Meadow didn't since Ramsay hurried off to meet up with one of the other police officers.

Fletcher reached them and gave them a tight smile. His face was still white as a sheet and he looked a little unsteady on his feet. He automatically crouched down and stroked Noo-noo absently. She licked his chin in response and he rubbed her again before standing up again, back ramrod-straight.

Meadow, never one to hold back, reached out and gave Fletcher a hug. "We are all just so sorry, Fletcher! Whatever is the world coming to?"

Miss Sissy gave a low growl and to cover it up, Beatrice hastily added, "We're so very sorry about Edie, Fletcher. She was incredibly kind earlier this morning when I was out walking my grandson. She invited us in to see your fish."

Fletcher gave her another smile and his eyes grew misty. He gave them an impatient rub with his hand. "That sounds just like Edie," he said gruffly. "Always looking for ways to lend someone a hand."

Beatrice said, "Ramsay thought you might be more comfortable if we waited at my house for them to finish up at your place. Would you like to go there?"

The alternative was watching the crime scene team work outside and inside his house before bringing Edie out on a stretcher. Beatrice didn't think it was a great option.

Fletcher hesitated a second before saying, "That would be good, thanks."

They walked back to Beatrice's house, Noo-noo leading the way. It was silent at first with no one really knowing what to say. Then Meadow, never one to be comfortable in silence, suddenly popped into action and started a rambling monologue about menu planning, grocery shopping, cooking, and gardening. For once, Beatrice wasn't sorry to hear her prattle on, although Miss Sissy appeared not to agree with her as she glowered at Meadow.

Beatrice unlocked the door and held it open for everyone. They filed in quietly, aside from Meadow.

"Food," barked Miss Sissy.

Beatrice latched onto this request, or possibly order, with relief. Yes, food would be good. Miss Sissy wouldn't be as grouchy with food. Meadow wouldn't be as chatty with her mouth full. And, perhaps, Fletcher wouldn't look as if he were about to pass out on the floor with a bite or so to eat.

"I'll pull something out," said Beatrice, hurrying toward the kitchen. "Everyone, please sit down."

Everyone did as Beatrice found some crackers and cheese, leftover pasta salad, a bit of fruit, and some cookies. She tossed a couple of treats to Noo-noo before placing the food on a tray with napkins, plates, and forks and putting it down on the coffee table in the living room. She snapped her fingers. "Drinks. I'll get everyone some water. Unless . . . maybe something stronger should be in order?"

Fletcher shook his head. "I'm okay, thanks."

"I'll get the waters," said Meadow quickly. Apparently, even Meadow had finally reached an end to the one-sided conversation she was having.

As Meadow was in the kitchen and Miss Sissy loaded her small plate with food, Beatrice leaned forward and gazed at Fletcher with concern. "Are you all right? Would you like me to bring you some aspirin or anything?"

He was rubbing his forehead absently, which is what made Beatrice think he had a headache coming on. He shook his head, though and gave her that faint smile again. "It's okay, thanks." He glanced at the tray of food as if surprised it had appeared there and then hesitantly picked up a couple of crackers.

Meadow came back with the drinks just in time to hear Fletcher mutter, "I really need to move."

Meadow's eyes grew wide as she thrust a water glass at him. "Move? From Dappled Hills?"

He nodded and then looked chagrined. "Nothing against the town, of course. It's just that there's nothing left for me here, now. Edie is gone. She was the one who was really spearheading getting the house and yard set up just the way we wanted it." His voice grew gruff again and he cleared it. "There's just no way that I can go back to living in that house as if nothing has happened."

Meadow said, "I know Ramsay will find out who did this, Fletcher. They won't get away with it! So if you're worried about your safety, just keep that in mind."

Fletcher shook his head. "That's really not it. I'm sure Ramsay will do a good job. It's more that my life here was started with a mutual vision that Edie and I had. Without her, there's just nothing I want to stay for. Edie and I were going to fix up the house and the yard. We were going to start a family and then Edie was going to spend time with the baby at home. We had all kinds of ideas for putting a swing set and a sandbox out in the backyard." His voice broke up a little at the end.

The whole idea of Fletcher being driven out of Dappled Hills by the recent events appeared to really upset Meadow.

"I am just *so sorry*, Fletcher! I simply can't imagine what's going on. Do you have any idea who might have done this to Edie? It's all just so crazy!" Meadow nearly knocked over her water glass until Beatrice reached out to save it.

Miss Sissy growled around the cookie in her mouth and Beatrice gave her a repressive look.

Fletcher shook his head. "I have no idea. Just like I didn't know who could have killed Petunia." He looked rather sick again as he mentioned Petunia's death. "I guess the two have got to be related, right?"

Beatrice said, "I guess they *must* be."

"It's a very safe place," stressed Meadow, still trying to sell Fletcher on Dappled Hills and its many excellent features, despite current evidence to the contrary.

Fletcher continued, "There is one thing. It's not really anything much. It's just that I keep thinking more about Petunia and Elspeth McDonald."

Beatrice's heart sank a little. She hated to think the older woman could possibly be involved in one death, let alone two. "Something happened between them?"

"Petunia was talking about it one morning and I should have paid better attention, but I was trying to get the equipment in the gym set up for the first PE class to come through. I do remember Petunia saying she and Elspeth had some kind of run-in."

Meadow frowned. "Elspeth doesn't seem like the kind of person to have run-ins."

Fletcher shrugged. "That's my word, it might not have been hers. Like I said, I wasn't listening as well as I should have been. Anyway, it had something to do with Elspeth professionally."

"Something to do with her teaching?" Beatrice set down her cookie. Her stomach was hurting a bit.

"That's right." He looked up at the ceiling as if the answer might be written up there. "Maybe it had something to do with her absentmindedness. Because she's gotten real absentminded. She left her car running in the school parking lot the other day for hours. I was leading a group of kids outside to run around the track and just happened to notice it." He paused and still studied the ceiling. Then he looked at them again. "Yep. That was definitely it. The state testing booklets."

Beatrice remembered Piper telling her about all of the protocol involved with the state tests of the students. "Those booklets have to be locked up, don't they?"

"They do. And Elspeth hadn't done that. Even worse, it looked like she'd opened them up and flipped through one of them. Petunia couldn't believe it. Elspeth has been at the school forever and it's not like she doesn't know the rules."

Meadow said slowly, "So you're saying that Elspeth was behaving unethically at school."

Fletcher picked up his glass and took a big swig of water. "I'm not saying anything. Petunia was telling me that. And I don't know if it qualifies as unethical or the actions of someone who's becoming confused."

Miss Sissy made a growling noise at the idea of being confused and Noo-noo growled softly, too, in sympathy.

Beatrice said, "Do you think if Elspeth felt she was being backed in a corner that she might be worried enough to have murdered Petunia?"

"That's the real question, isn't it? And I don't really know. I have a hard time picturing it, but desperate people do desperate things," said Fletcher.

"Was Petunia going to tell the principal about Elspeth?" asked Meadow.

Fletcher said, "Yeah. But first, she told Elspeth. She wanted to give her a chance to just go ahead and retire before Petunia said anything to the administration. I think Petunia thought that would be a way for her to save face. Elspeth could use all kinds of excuses for retiring. For one thing, she's way over the age of retirement. And I know Elspeth told me her daughter is going to be moving to town. She could have told the principal that she wanted to spend more time with her."

"But in the middle of the school year? Wouldn't it have been hard to find someone to teach the kids?" asked Meadow.

Fletcher shook his head. "We have a few really good substitute teachers and several of them are retired teachers or teachers who left full-time work to start a family. There would have been some really good options for subs to finish out the school year."

Meadow looked as if she might want to unpack that, but Fletcher abruptly stood up from the table, restlessly going to the window and looking out.

"I'm going to walk back over there and see what's going on and what they're doing. Maybe Ramsay has more information he can give me if they've been able to find anything out."

Beatrice stood, too. "Do you think you'll be able to stay over there tonight? Might the police still be working over there late? You could stay here—we have a guest room. It's tiny, but it's functional and you're certainly welcome to stay."

Fletcher reached down to give Noo-noo a rub and she leaned against his legs as he did. "I'm guessing they're going to be over there pretty late. I'm going to get them to grab me some stuff and head to a hotel for the night. Thanks for the offer, though—I appreciate it. Right now, I want a little time to be alone and think things through."

Meadow looked at his plate. There were a couple of half-eaten crackers there. "You didn't really eat, Fletcher. Don't you need to have something?"

Miss Sissy narrowed her eyes at him as if finding people who didn't eat very suspicious.

He shook his head again and his face was etched with exhaustion. "I just don't have the appetite, sorry."

Beatrice hesitated for a moment and then said, "By the way, Fletcher, Piper mentioned she'd seen Edie at the school yesterday when I was there picking her up. Did she give you a ride home?"

Fletcher shook his head absently. "No. Funny, I was just talking about Elspeth being absentminded and I'm apparently the same way. I forgot something at home and had to call Edie to bring it to me at the school." He headed for the door. "Thanks again. I appreciate it." And with that, he took his leave.

Chapter Nine

Meadow said, "Well. I'm just not sure what to think about any of this."

"I know," said Beatrice. "At least Fletcher seemed to be in better shape emotionally when he left."

"I mean I don't know what to think about the fact that he wants to move from Dappled Hills. Can you imagine? I think he should just put the house for sale and then find another spot to live. Dappled Hills is the best!" She frowned. "Do you think he's the kind of guy who might fit into our quilting guild? Ash is practically an honorary member now and I'd really like to grow our male membership."

Beatrice's head started hurting. "Meadow, I really don't think this is the best time to engage in guild recruitment. Fletcher obviously has a lot on his mind right now and maybe it would be best for him to get a fresh start somewhere else, like he was saying."

"Bad man," offered Miss Sissy. She had cookie crumbs dotting the top of her long, floral dress.

Meadow said, "Is this about the argument you said he had with Edie again? Because you know every couple fights, don't you?"

Miss Sissy glowered at her. She might well have *not* known this since she'd never found quite the right man to settle down with.

Meadow persisted, "It's true. Why, Ramsay and I argued this morning over whose turn it was to walk Boris. And it was most definitely *his* turn. I know Ramsay keeps talking about retirement, but I wonder what I'm going to do with him at home all day long. I mean, I *love* Ramsay. I do! But I simply don't want to spend all day with him." She frowned and looked at her watch. "Goodness. I believe it's time for me to walk Boris *now*. The vet has him on a special diet and exercise regimen. I'm doing so much walking, though that I'm starting to feel like I'm the one on the diet."

"Has Boris gained that much weight?" asked Beatrice. She'd seen their huge beast of a dog just a few days earlier but had been mainly focused on the animal's dirty paws at the time since Boris appeared to be aiming them at her clean khakis.

Meadow sighed. "I'm afraid so. I do believe it may have something to do with Will's affection for Cheerios cereal. I'm starting to wonder if Will isn't dropping those Cheerios from his highchair on purpose. He does tend to squeal and laugh hysterically when he does it." Meadow looked thoughtful.

"Supper?" asked Miss Sissy with a hopeful lilt to her voice. Meadow was now cooking and bringing supper several times a week to both Piper and Ash and Miss Sissy after they'd discovered Miss Sissy ate nothing but greens of various sorts when she wasn't getting meals. Although Beatrice was beginning to think that diet of greens might be responsible for Miss Sissy's longevity and lack of pressing health issues.

"Absolutely! It's fish bake tonight. And you two remember the guild meeting tomorrow, please. We definitely need good attendance so everyone can figure out how to stop Dora from wrecking our quilt show when she's there to update us on her plans. Toodle-loo!"

Miss Sissy's face froze at the mention of fish and, when Meadow was safely out the door, she made a face. "Bleh. Fish."

Beatrice said, "You know everything Meadow cooks ends up tasting absolutely amazing. It'll probably have all kinds of Ritz cracker buttery topping or sit on asparagus or something like that."

Meadow's mention of Dora had gotten Beatrice thinking. She glanced over at Miss Sissy, who was still looking rather unhappy about her upcoming supper. "By the way, Miss Sissy, you know you don't have to do anything you don't want to do . . . right?"

"Like eat fish?" asked the old woman with alacrity.

"I was thinking more about church. I know Dora was speaking with you about different ways to get more involved there and I couldn't tell if that was something you were interested in or not. She definitely seems to have plans to recruit you into choir."

Miss Sissy shrugged. Beatrice said, "I know you've been a little at loose ends lately, what with not being able to drive and all. Of course you should consider Dora's idea, too. But I wondered if you might want to help some with the quilt show next week, which is something else Dora mentioned. It's a shorter-term commitment than choir and you'd be perfect at setting-up. You can help label every quilt with a number and get the quilter's name and phone number on a registration form. You can even give us a hand with setting up the quilt racks for some of the smaller quilts and hanging the quilts with clothespins or men's pant hangers—with the smaller quilts you won't have to get on a stepstool. And it would be great if you could help with working the door and taking everyone's two dollars when they come in and handing them a program."

Miss Sissy tilted her head to the side like a bird as she thought it through. Then she smiled and nodded. She looked pleased at being asked to do more than just show up at the quilt show.

"Great! And you can give us a hand during the quilt show, too. We're going to have a raffle for one of June Bug's quilts and you can pick the winning entry."

Miss Sissy's smile grew even wider.

"Good. We could definitely use the extra hands." She picked up the tray and the plates and took them into the kitchen to wash up.

Miss Sissy abruptly seemed to have had enough visiting. While Beatrice was running the water in the kitchen sink, she heard the front door close with a bang. She quickly dried off her hands with a dish towel and looked out the door. Miss Sissy was walking away.

"See you later," Beatrice opened the door and called to the old woman and she held a hand up in response, never turning around. When she had her mind set on something, there was no changing it.

Alone again with Noo-noo, Beatrice finished the washing up and then settled down with her book for a while. By the time Wyatt came back from work, she was feeling relaxed and rested again.

Wyatt gave her a quick hug and lifted up a brown paper bag. "Thought I'd pick up Chinese takeout for supper tonight . . . I just got our usual orders. Sorry, I should have checked to see if you'd fixed anything first."

Beatrice shook her head. "No, and that sounds great. I was starting to think we might have grilled cheese sandwiches and tomato soup for supper. My day got derailed and I never really managed to make a plan for what we'd eat."

Wyatt frowned as he started unpacking the containers. "Did something happen? I know you texted me earlier to see if I was free, but you didn't mention what was going on."

Beatrice filled him in as Wyatt stopped unpacking and sat down to listen more carefully to her.

"That's awful," he said quietly.

"I know. And when I spoke to her earlier, she seemed so enthusiastic about helping out with the music ministry and getting the chance to play. It's just so sad."

Wyatt said in a grim voice, "I'm starting to wonder if we need more locks on the door," he said. "That's a little too close to home."

"It must be all related to what happened to Petunia. It would be weird if it weren't." Beatrice went into the kitchen and returned with two plates and then returned for two glasses of sweet tea. "Although I can't really figure out why anyone would murder Edie. If she knew something about what happened to Petunia, it would make sense that the killer would want to silence her. But I don't understand how she'd know that—it's not as if she worked at the school. Although it does sound like she was there yesterday morning to bring something to Fletcher."

Wyatt slowly opened the takeout containers and watched as Beatrice used a serving spoon to divide out the rice and entrees. "Does Ramsay have any idea what's going on yet?"

"I haven't really spoken to him, except to give him information on what happened when we found Edie. But I've heard a few things along the way."

"Like what?" Wyatt took a forkful of his stir-fry as Noo-noo watched hopefully from the floor.

"Well, Petunia appeared to really make waves even though she was here for just a short time. Sterling Wade apparently had quite a crush on her, as I mentioned to you earlier. Do you know him well?"

Wyatt shook his head. "Not really, although I know he's been helping out with the youth programs at the church."

"No; although it appears that Sterling was knocking himself out to start a relationship with Petunia. From everything I've heard, though, she was really out of his league. At least, that's what Fletcher was saying. From what I understand, Sterling is pretty awkward except around kids, and Petunia was anything but."

Wyatt said, "But why would Sterling murder Petunia if he was so fond of her?"

"I guess the thinking is that maybe after being rejected too much, he snapped and let his frustration out on her," said Beatrice with a shrug. She hesitated. "I've also picked up on some vibes from Fletcher. I was wondering if maybe he was having an affair with Petunia. Or if they were starting to become involved."

Wyatt winced. "That would have been devastating for Edie, if she'd known about it."

Beatrice nodded. "I'm sure it would have. And again, it's not like I really know anything, but I just had a sneaking suspicion that Fletcher and Petunia might have been involved. Fletcher did seem really upset about Edie. He came over here for a while because the police were investigating at his house. He was talking about leaving Dappled Hills. I really got the impression that it wasn't just because he lost his wife but that he felt as if he'd lost *everything*. And, if he had a relationship with Petunia and lost both Petunia and Edie just days apart, that makes sense."

Wyatt said, "It seems like Edie would have had the most motive for murdering Petunia, doesn't it? Except now she's dead, as well."

"And we have no idea if she knew anything about Fletcher and Petunia or even if there really *was* a Fletcher and Petunia." She paused. "And then there's Elspeth. I hate to say it because I know how involved she is with the church, but it's starting to look as if she had a motive, herself."

Wyatt sighed. "I hate to hear that. I just called Elspeth's daughter earlier today. I felt uncomfortable doing it, sort of like I was betraying Elspeth in the process. I told her daughter I was making the call out of concern for her but was hoping I hadn't stepped out of bounds."

"What did she say?"

Wyatt said, "She seemed grateful that I'd told her Elspeth seemed to be having memory problems. She said it was hard to really tell from long distance. But you were saying Elspeth might have a motive for Petunia's death?"

Beatrice sighed. "It sure looks that way. Two different people have told me about an altercation between Elspeth and Petunia. It seems like it may have had something to do with the fact that Elspeth is having memory issues and is probably trying to keep it under wraps. Fletcher told me Elspeth even left her car running in the teachers' parking lot the other day. I'm really glad you made that phone call to her daughter and so relieved she's coming to live here."

"I think it will be better for Elspeth to have family here to help her out, for sure. So there was some sort of incident at school that Petunia brought up?"

Beatrice said, "From what I understand. Possibly something to do with the state test booklets. Anyway, Fletcher overheard them arguing. I suppose it's possible that Elspeth could have felt desperate to keep Petunia quiet so she wouldn't lose her job. I think she really identifies as being a teacher and loves the kids and doesn't want to give it up."

They sat quietly for a few moments. Wyatt said slowly, "Teaching has always seemed to be something Elspeth loved and was proud of doing. It must have been hard to think about that being taken away from her."

Beatrice sighed again. "And then there's Dora."

"Dora Tucker?" Wyatt's face was unhappy. It must seem to him that half his best volunteers at the church were murder suspects.

"That's right. Elspeth told me that Dora was having a difference of opinion with Petunia recently, although she didn't want to offer any details."

Wyatt took a mouthful of food and thought about this for a minute.

Beatrice added, "Dora does like doing things her way, though. If Petunia didn't completely understand that, they may have bumped heads. I know Dora didn't expect any disagreement at all when she proposed major changes to the quilt show next week."

Wyatt raised his eyebrows at this. "Uh-oh. Major changes? That sounds like trouble. I have the feeling Meadow wasn't happy about that."

"Not in the slightest. Knowing Meadow, she's likely planning a coup. Anyway, she has some sort of plan to push back. Lots of drama lately."

There was a tentative knock on the door and Wyatt and Beatrice looked at each other in surprise.

"Meadow?" suggested Wyatt.

"No way. You know how Meadow's knocks are. You definitely know it's her from the pounding." Beatrice often felt an echoing pounding in her head in response to thinking about Meadow's knocks.

Wyatt quickly rubbed his mouth with a napkin and hurried to the door.

Chapter Ten

Elspeth McDonald was there, holding a basket of home-grown tomatoes and looking abashed. She could see Beatrice and their food on the table from the door. "Oh goodness," she said. "I should have called first. You're eating your supper."

Wyatt, polite as always, stepped aside and said, "Come on in and join us, Elspeth. I picked up a ton of food. It's just take-out, nothing fancy."

Beatrice felt a little less generous, not being fond of people dropping by unexpectedly, especially during meals, but she managed a tight smile.

"These tomatoes look wonderful, Elspeth," said Wyatt warmly. "Beatrice and I love tomato sandwiches, but we didn't plant any tomatoes this year."

Elspeth beamed at him. "I know just what you mean. Spring is always such a busy time, isn't it? There's so much going on that planting tomatoes seems to slip by. I actually put a reminder on my calendar this year so I wouldn't forget."

Beatrice said, "That's a good idea. I'll have to do that next spring. Of course, then when considerate people like you come in, I don't miss out on tomatoes and it becomes less of a priority!" She gestured to the boxes of Chinese takeaway. "Would you like some stir-fry, Elspeth? Or maybe some fried rice?"

Elspeth shook her head. "I've already eaten, but thanks. I'd love a glass of water, if I could, though."

Beatrice fixed that and brought it back to the table. Elspeth's face was pink with happiness as she spoke with Wyatt about some of the upcoming programs at the church. Although she was perfectly polite to Beatrice when she returned with the water, Beatrice had the distinct impression Elspeth wasn't at all pleased that she was there and preferred to have Wyatt all to herself. She gave Wyatt a wry smile. This was a phenomenon she'd experienced before with various ladies of the church.

After a few minutes of chatting and after Wyatt and Beatrice had finished eating, Elspeth said slowly, "I did want to bring you the tomatoes, but there has been something on my mind that's been worrying me. I wondered if I could speak with you about Petunia." She flushed. "And Edie, too. I just heard about her death from one of my neighbors."

Wyatt nodded solemnly. "Beatrice was filling me in shortly before you arrived. I was so sorry to hear of it. Of course, you know Petunia from the school, so it must be especially hard for you, Elspeth. And I'm imagining you knew Edie from church."

Elspeth swallowed and then said, "Not really, but still, it's very hard. I did enjoy the beautiful music at church several weeks ago and I know Edie was the director that morning. Such wickedness afoot with two young women dead now. I was still at the school when I heard about Edie . . . just trying to wrap things up there, you know. It's been so very busy between school and the church."

Wyatt said gently, "If your volunteer work at the church gets to be too much, don't worry about letting me or anyone else there know. We can always recruit someone to step in. We've really appreciated all you've done for the church, especially working as hard as you are."

Elspeth beamed at him. "Oh, no. No, I love keeping busy. And working around the youth, especially on Wednesday nights. It's a real joy for me. My problem is that I need to figure out a way to fit in everything *else* I need to do. Scheduling a physical, for one thing. I keep meaning to go to the doctor, but I've put it off."

"That's exactly the kind of thing Wyatt means," said Beatrice softly. "He wants to make sure you make time for necessary tasks like taking care of your health, even if it means someone else needs to cover for your volunteering."

Elspeth narrowed her eyes at Beatrice as if not appreciating the interjection. Beatrice decided it might be best to keep quiet and let Wyatt do the talking for them.

Elspeth apparently decided a change of subject was in order. "Beatrice, I understand you were on the scene when Edie was found."

The way Elspeth said it, it made it sound as if Beatrice had something to do with Edie's death. And here she found herself being pulled into conversation again, just when she decided it might be wise to let Wyatt have the floor.

"I was. Miss Sissy and I were taking Noo-noo on a walk at the time," said Beatrice mildly.

Elspeth bobbed her head. "I see. I know she and Fletcher live practically next door to you."

Beatrice raised her eyebrows. "Yes. I didn't realize you were acquainted enough to know where she lived. Did you ever visit there?"

Elspeth turned a deep purple, obviously regretting that she'd said anything at all. "No, no, of course not. I suppose I must have picked up their address when speaking with Fletcher at some point. I know he'd mentioned to me that it was a new house for them. He seemed really excited about it when they were moving in."

"It's a pity you didn't see it. They were doing so much work in there. I'd taken my grandson on a stroller ride earlier that day and Edie invited us in to see their fish. Will was absolutely enchanted by them. She seemed like such a gentle person. It's terrible that she's gone just as she and Fletcher were embarking on a new life at their new home.

Elspeth pressed her lips together and looked down at the floor.

Wyatt said in a comforting way, "I'm sure Ramsay will find out who's behind this very soon."

Elspeth looked up again. "I hope so. It's just awful. And I can't really feel safe at home all by myself. I had some new locks installed at my house and I swear I was on the point of buying a large dog before I talked myself out of it. Such unsettling times."

She looked flustered again and stood up abruptly. "I'm sorry again that I disturbed your supper."

Beatrice and Wyatt both made dismissive sounds. "Feel free to come over anytime," said Wyatt warmly while Beatrice shot him a sideways look. It was the last thing Beatrice wanted, but it made Elspeth smile.

Elspeth gave Noo-noo a couple of kisses and took her leave, carefully closing the door behind her.

Wyatt gave Beatrice a rueful look. "She was absolutely lucid in every way."

"That's the thing, though. It's possible, as you know, to have good days and bad days. And it's not as if her bad days were reported by a single person—there were several people who've mentioned Elspeth's memory problems. Actually, her entire Bible study was worried about her, from what I've heard. You did the right thing, speaking with her daughter."

Wyatt rubbed the back of his neck. "I hope so." He smiled at Beatrice. "Maybe we should talk about something else. Anything interesting going on?"

Beatrice grinned back at him. "Well, I have an upcoming, likely-contentious guild meeting tomorrow."

Wyatt groaned. "You're not even getting a break from stress at your quilt guild? I thought it was one of the most relaxing things you did."

"Ordinarily, it definitely is. We have snacks and we catch up with each other, and we share what we've been working on. But this time Dora is popping in to give an update on our preparations for the quilt show." Beatrice grimaced.

"Got it. And Dora's making all the radical changes that Meadow is planning on sabotaging."

"Something like that." Beatrice stretched and then reached out to pick up some of the takeout containers. "Look, we have enough for lunch tomorrow."

They cleared up the dishes and then Wyatt said, "What are you planning on doing now?"

"I don't think we should do anything productive at all. I won't quilt or clean. You won't work on anything for the church. We should have a glass of wine and watch a movie that classifies as pure entertainment with very little redeeming value."

Which is exactly what they did.

The next afternoon, Beatrice was getting ready to head to the guild meeting when there was a tap at the door and Noo-noo exploded into joyful barking. Beatrice chuckled and reached down to give the little dog a rub. Judging from her reaction, it must be Ramsay at the door.

Sure enough, Ramsay greeted her with a tired smile as she opened the door. Noo-noo, knowing she shouldn't jump but badly wanting to, had a case of the wiggles and finally flung her corgi self on the floor for a tummy rub.

"What a good girl," crooned Ramsay. He gave Beatrice a rueful look. "Want to come over and train Boris not to jump on guests?"

Beatrice snorted. "Just like you to try to assign me with an impossible task. You know Boris has a mind of his own."

Ramsay gave Noo-noo a final rub and then reached into his pocket as Noo-noo looked on expectantly. "Here you are, girl," he said, tossing her a dog treat. He said to Beatrice, "I've been trying to do a little training with Boris, so I always have treats on hand. It doesn't seem to be taking."

Beatrice noticed how weary Ramsay looked. "Here, come sit down. You look bushed. Haven't you been able to get any sleep?"

"Not the amount I need to, apparently. I tell you, Beatrice, I think my days in law enforcement are drawing to a close. I've been watching those young guys from the state police and they just seem so much fresher and more energized than I do. And sharper." He said the last a bit sadly.

"Now, I doubt that's true. Maybe they're just eager to prove themselves. And you don't have anything to prove. You've been an important part of this community for decades and you don't have to be hungry for success or promotion."

Ramsay winced. "Promotion? Definitely not. What I'd like is to be *de*-moted . . . to be totally retired and just reading books all day. I've got a good one now that's really different. *The One-in-a-Million Boy*. Nice story about a boy forging an unlikely friendship with a 104-year old woman."

"I'll have to add it to my to-be-read list, although the way that list is going, it will be a while until I get to it. I swear I'm not a slow reader, but somehow I've ended up with a stack of books to read lately."

Ramsay said, "Well, considering everything that's gone on lately, I'm surprised you've had the time or the energy to read at all. You doing okay after finding Edie?"

I nodded. "That was a shocker. Like I told you, I'd *just* seen her earlier that afternoon. She was full of life and working in her yard. I could tell she was proud of the new house. And Fletcher was saying that the two of them had made all sorts of plans for a life together. It's all just such a shame."

Ramsay nodded solemnly. "I know. That's what's motivating me to keep going with this case. I feel terrible for her and her family—so much time ahead of her, so much to look forward to. And to be taken out that way is awful."

"Do you have any idea why she was targeted? Is her death related to Petunia's?"

Ramsay said slowly, "We don't really know right now, although I'm obviously leaning toward the idea that the deaths are somehow related. After all, she was connected to the school through her husband. To me, it all seems to be revolving around the school, although I haven't really figured out exactly why. I know you hear a lot of bits and pieces as you're out and about. Have you heard anything that might help out?"

Beatrice shook her head. "I've heard things, but I'm not exactly sure how they fit in. You might have heard a lot of the same things, yourself. I'm thinking there was some sort of love triangle going on."

Ramsay raised his eyebrows. "A *triangle*? I only know of a failed connection between Sterling and Petunia. That Sterling was hoping to have a relationship with Petunia and that she wasn't interested. There was someone else involved?"

"I don't *know* that, but it's something I suspect. Fletcher's reaction when he found Petunia made me wonder. And Piper thought there might be something between them."

Ramsay said slowly, "So Fletcher and Petunia had a thing together . . . possibly. That does give Edie a motive, but she's a victim, herself."

"That's what I was struggling with, too. But I wondered if maybe Edie had somehow either been driving by the school or been at the school and had seen what happened."

Ramsay frowned. "Okay, but why not say something? Why not call the police right away?"

"What if she *did* know that her husband and Petunia were having an affair? Maybe she didn't feel motivated to help the police find the murderer. Or it could be that she wasn't really sure exactly what she saw, but she was spotted by the killer. Or maybe she decided she wanted to blackmail the murderer because she and Fletcher were low on funds and had a lot of future plans."

Ramsay rubbed his eyes wearily. "Yep. All of those might be reasons why she was killed."

Beatrice said cautiously, "But remember that I don't have any actual proof of a relationship between Fletcher and Petunia. It definitely wasn't out in the open, if there was one. You might want to tread carefully with that if you speak with Fletcher."

Ramsay nodded and stood up, reaching down to rub Noo-noo as she gave him a beseeching look. "Sorry, girl, got to go."

Beatrice glanced at the wall clock and said, "Oh gosh, I need to run, too. Over to your house, as a matter of fact."

"The guild meeting," said Ramsay with a chuckle. "You'd better hurry. I heard an earful last night from Meadow telling me how you were going to help somehow corral Dora into doing whatever Meadow wants with the quilt show."

"Right, ha. Not a chance of that, but I like her optimism."

Ramsay spoke over his shoulder as he headed toward the door. "Beatrice, I appreciate your insights and your sharing them with me. Helps me think outside the box a little. Take care now and keep in touch if you hear anything else."

Chapter Eleven

Minutes later, Beatrice hurried out for the guild meeting. Meadow and Ramsay's house was actually a renovated barn with lofty beams above and a beautiful wooden floor. There were lots of signs that a baby spent a good deal of time in the house. There were toys and baby equipment everywhere, pushed to the walls to make room for the quilters and for their guest, Dora. As always, Meadow had gone the extra mile with the food she'd prepared.

Beatrice gaped at the counter heaped with serving plates and bowls of fried chicken, greens, mashed potatoes, and biscuits. "Meadow, have you made supper for the entire guild? Now when it's at my house, I'll feel bad about putting out a cheese platter and some fruit."

Meadow chuckled. "Well, you know how I am when I get anxious about things. It's just good to stay busy. First I was just making supper for Ramsay and me, Miss Sissy, and Piper and Ash. Then I realized I could just keep going because it felt so good to cook. So I went *back* to the store and picked up more food and then set about to cooking it. Everybody can bring some home for their dinner tonight if they want to."

Miss Sissy had walked over early and was now perched on the sofa with a large plate of food. She didn't seem at all worried that she'd be eating the exact same thing for supper. Meadow plopped down next to her to chat and Miss Sissy grunted from time to time, concentrating on her food as Meadow kept up her monologue.

Posy came up to Beatrice and said sympathetically, "I heard what happened yesterday. I'm so sorry! What a terrible thing. Poor Edie. I didn't know her well, but she seemed so lovely when I'd speak with her at church. And she was so very talented—playing all those instruments."

"Isn't it awful? And the sad thing was that Edie had been so warm and welcoming to Miss Sissy, Will, and me when we were there earlier for a walk. She was so vital, so full of life. It was hard for me to wrap my head around the fact that she was gone."

Georgia Simpson came up to join them and overheard Beatrice. She looked sad. "I just hate all this. I guess these two deaths must somehow be connected, right? There just couldn't be two unrelated murders in Dappled Hills. It wouldn't make sense." She paused and asked quietly, "How was Fletcher? Did you see him?"

Beatrice said, "Devastated, for sure. He was already upset over Petunia's death since he'd known her from school and this seemed like another terrible blow. He was talking about moving away and setting up a new life somewhere else. I don't think he's interested in staying in their house."

Posy's sweet face saddened and Georgia said, "I feel terrible for him. I hope he takes some time off and lets the school hire a sub for his gym classes."

"Is that the kind of thing you think he'd do?" asked Beatrice. "I don't really know him, but it seems to me he's more the kind of person who'd want to stay busy."

Posy nodded. "Sometimes keeping distracted is a good thing."

Georgia said with a sigh, "You're right. I don't think he *is* the kind of person who'd take a break from school and spend time sorting out his feelings. I like Fletcher, but he's more of a man's man type. I think he goes hunting in the fall, has a punching bag for workouts, does fly-fishing, and that kind of thing."

"The rugged kind," said Posy.

"Exactly. I've had plenty of conversations with Fletcher but never really felt I got into his head at all. He's the type of guy to keep his feelings under wraps. I think it's amazing he opened up enough to you to tell you what he was thinking," said Georgia.

Beatrice shrugged. "I think he was in shock, honestly, and trying to work out what his next steps are."

"Is he considered a suspect?" asked Georgia with concern.

"I'm sure he must be. Spouses are always the main suspects, aren't they? But he says he was at school. And he did drive up to the house while Miss Sissy and I were there with Ramsay."

Posy said, "I just can't imagine anyone doing something like this, especially someone we know! Georgia, do you think it could be someone at the school?"

"It makes sense, doesn't it? Or at least, it's someone associated with the school somehow. Although it's really hard for me to picture anyone I work with doing something like this. They're all the sort of people who care for children all day, after all. Fletcher has always seemed like a really upright guy. He goes the extra mile for the teachers, too. I've seen him jump-start a coworker's car and help teachers move heavy stuff in their class-rooms. I mean, he's not the warm and cuddly type of guy—more really efficient and usually kind of stoic. But he'll do anything for you. Somehow he doesn't really seem the wife-murdering type." Georgia gave a little shudder at the thought.

Posy somberly shook her head. "Now Fletcher needs some-one to go the extra mile for *him*, the poor man."

Georgia nodded. "A bunch of us at the school are organizing meals for him. We know he eats really healthy stuff, so we're go-ing to have to forego the usual lasagna pans and things like that. We have a signup sheet. Maybe that will make *something* a little easier for him."

Beatrice asked, "I keep hearing things about Elspeth and Sterling and their interactions with Petunia. What are your im-pressions of them?"

"Oh, I like both of them because they're so great with chil-dren. Elspeth has been teaching for forever and she's got almost a sixth sense when it comes to her students. She can tell when they're having a rough day and she's able to defuse them before they really unravel. If they forget their lunch money or their lunchbox, she spots them for it. Sterling is really knowledgeable and always seems to be someone the kids go to with whatever is on their minds. He has a great rapport with the students. Al-though maybe not as great of a rapport with adults." Georgia looked rueful.

Beatrice said, "I understand Sterling might have had some-thing of a crush on Petunia?"

Georgia said ruefully, “I think Sterling has had a crush on a lot of people.” She had a tinge of pink in her cheeks.

Posy’s eyes opened wide. “You, too?”

“It was nothing,” said Georgia quickly. “Way before I started even dating Tony. I was totally surprised when he asked me out. I told him at the time that I didn’t think it was a great idea—we were coworkers, after all. Besides, he really wasn’t my type.”

Savannah, Georgia’s sister, joined them with a plate of food. She clucked over the mention of Sterling. “Some people don’t know when to give up.”

Beatrice asked, “Was he really persistent?”

Savannah chimed in before Georgia could answer. “Georgia’s too nice to say so, but he *was*. You remember, Georgia. Sterling would pop by our house and say he was just passing by and then we’d feel forced to offer him supper. He’d always corner Georgia at school.”

“I don’t know if I used the word *corner*,” said Georgia.

“You did,” said Savannah promptly. “And he would. You’d come back home from school and say that you were minding your own business, trying to watch the kids on the playground at recess and he’d suddenly appear out of nowhere and force you into a conversation.”

Georgia gave Savannah a fond smile. “You were always very protective of me.” She looked at Posy and Beatrice. “It wasn’t *that* bad. He’d talk to me about his day and ask about mine or talk about how things were when we were kids and how different things are now. But the thing was, I was trying to really watch my kids and I always felt a little distracted.”

Savannah continued looking unimpressed with her sister's defense of Sterling. She gave her final argument to support Sterling's pushiness. "Plus, he gave Georgia inappropriate gifts."

This made Posy's eyes grow even wider than they'd been before.

Georgia chuckled. "Not what you might think. He gave me a locket with a picture of him in it."

Savannah shook her head. "Just like I said—inappropriate. That's the sort of gift a boyfriend gives a girlfriend, not a coworker."

"I have to agree with Savannah on that one," said Beatrice. "Sterling shouldn't have done it. It was unprofessional."

Georgia said sadly, "I sort of felt sorry for him at the time. He was trying so hard to win me over. And I couldn't have been less-interested. I remember that I tried to think of someone he might be a good match with."

"To foist him off on someone else," said Savannah with a nod.

Georgia laughed. "Not *foist*. I just thought there should be someone who'd be a better choice of companion than I was. But I couldn't think of anyone. It's a small town, after all, and there aren't a ton of choices to start out with."

"Like I mentioned, he didn't know when to give up," said Savannah. "Thank heaven you ended up with someone reasonable, like Tony."

Savannah was very fond of Tony. Not only did he very competently fix things at her house whenever she had any sort of problem, he also often invited her over to dinner with him and Georgia. He made her feel very much a part of their family.

Posy's voice got low. "What about poor Elspeth? I understand she's been in the suspect spotlight, too."

Georgia nodded. "I think that's making her especially agitated. She had to come back to the school yesterday because she forgot her tote bag that had all the work she needed to grade. She seemed really flustered and embarrassed when I saw her come back for it. And the bag had her cell phone in there too, I think."

"She left home to go back to the school?" asked Beatrice.

"Yes, she left early yesterday because she had a terrible headache. I helped watch her class for her, actually. Then she ended up having to come back to school after all."

This wasn't what Elspeth had told Wyatt and Beatrice last night. She'd understood that she'd been getting caught up with things at school. Was that a deliberate fib or just her poor memory at work?

Georgia, apparently uneasy about talking too much about her coworkers, quickly broached another subject and Posy was happily talking about the new birdhouses she'd made, the quilting project she was working on, and the new fabrics she'd gotten in at the shop. She said, "It's been good to be busy because Cork has been out of town visiting an old high school friend."

Savannah, always the pragmatist, said with a frown, "You've been keeping your doors and windows locked at night, haven't you? With Petunia and Edie, I've been especially vigilant, living alone as I do."

Posy nodded quickly, "I've been very careful about it. I'm going to sound like a baby, but with everything going on, I've been very skittish at night. I thought I was going to jump out of my skin last night when I heard a thump across the room, but it was just the cat jumping off the sofa."

"I bet Maisie was surprised when you jumped," chuckled Georgia.

"She jumped in response to my jump, and she's usually so laid back and not skittish at all," said Posy with a laugh. She added hesitantly, "I don't suppose any of you would like to come over and hang out at my house for a while tonight and keep me company, would you? Just long enough to take up some time in the evening before it's time to turn in. Cork comes back tomorrow and so it's the last night I'm home alone." Her face brightened. "We could watch a movie and eat spicy food that Cork can't eat."

"A girls' night in!" said Georgia. "I'd actually love that. Tony has to work late tonight, so I was going to be on my own anyway. I'd much rather hang out with y'all than be by myself."

"And I'd appreciate a change of scenery," said Savannah. "Maybe I can even bring some hand-piecing along to work on."

Beatrice said, "I think it sounds like fun. With everything going on, I could use a night that was just relaxing."

Posy looked delighted. "I'll make plans. Should we pick a musical or a costume drama? Or something completely different?"

Savannah said thoughtfully, "I don't think I've ever watched a musical, actually."

"Never?" asked Posy, raising her eyebrows in surprise. "Not even when you were a kid?"

Savannah looked at Georgia. "Did I? Do you remember?"

Georgia said, "You were more interested in doing other things than watching TV. I'd be watching *Grease* and you were organizing the towels in the linen closet."

Beatrice said, "We should get you caught up to speed, Savannah. There are a slew of really great musicals out there. Some are real classics like *The Sound of Music* or *Singing in the Rain* and then there are new classics like *Hamilton* or *Mamma Mia.*"

Posy was still unwilling to believe that Savannah had never seen a musical. "You didn't even watch *The Wizard of Oz*?"

Savannah shook her head and gave her gruff laugh. "I'm starting to realize there might be a gap in my education."

Posy gave them all a very serious, considering look. "I think we have to go with *The Wizard of Oz*. Or *Mary Poppins*."

Beatrice nodded solemnly. "It would be a shame not to."

Georgia said, "I think Savannah might really enjoy *The Wizard of Oz*. Plus, it's always a nice escape whenever I watch it and I could use an escape after this past week. Would that work for everybody?"

"It's a classic," said Beatrice simply. "I'd love to watch it again."

Posy beamed at them. "It's a plan. And I'll have Italian food for us to eat since it gives Cork terrible heartburn, but I love it."

Meadow's front door suddenly banged shut behind someone and they turned to see Dora Tucker there, singing out a greeting to the group, her frizzy hair gloriously uncombed. She strode over to join Edgenora, presumably to discuss some church-related business.

Savannah's eyes narrowed. "What's Dora doing here at a Village Quilters meeting? She's from the Cut-Ups guild."

Beatrice grimaced. "Dora is here to update us all on the quilt show final preparations and where we stand. I think there might be signups involved, too."

Posy gave Beatrice a confused look. "But why couldn't you do that? You're the co-chair."

"Dora would like to consider herself as in charge of the entire thing," said Beatrice wryly. "And, to be fair, she pretty much *has* been in charge of it all. At least she's trying to keep us in the loop as to the plans she's made."

Savannah's mouth drooped. "This is why I didn't want to be on the planning committee. And you know how I love to plan. I knew Dora wouldn't take kindly to input from anyone else."

Beatrice knew that Savannah did indeed enjoy planning. She was incredibly organized and tended to map out all the tasks for an event into a paper planner and then meticulously work through them, frequently getting a week ahead in the process. Georgia hadn't been kidding when she'd talked about how Savannah spent her free time organizing the linen closet. However, Beatrice also knew that Savannah wasn't the most flexible person in the world. The changes Dora proposed would have really thrown her off-balance. It was just as well she wasn't involved.

Dora left her conversation with Edgenora and headed over to Beatrice. The other women quickly dispersed, hurrying off to speak with various members of the guild. Dora grinned at Beatrice, her teeth looking very sharp and dangerous. Beatrice was tall, but Dora was even slightly taller and Beatrice felt as if she were looming down on her. "Good to see you, Beatrice. I'm so excited to share our plans for the show with your guild." She glanced around her, eyes alert as she took in the skylights with the sun beaming down from the soaring ceiling and the quilts scattered over every available wall and piece of furniture. "This is the first time I've been in Meadow's house."

"Is it?" asked Beatrice. She wasn't too surprised Meadow hadn't invited her over until now since Meadow hadn't seemed like a big fan of Dora's.

"It is." Dora paused. "It's very interesting."

Beatrice had the feeling that the rambling, somewhat chaotic nature of the quilts was very different from what the ultra-organized Dora would have in hers. She envisioned quilts displayed in a very methodical manner, perhaps by pattern or by color.

"Anyway," said Dora, "Like I said, it will be good to fill everyone in on our plans for the show so they'll know what to expect. I also brought signup sheets for the refreshment table and check-in and that sort of thing."

Beatrice raised her eyebrows. "They're really mostly your plans, Dora. Be sure to give yourself credit for it all." Particularly since she didn't want to be blamed for anything she hadn't had a hand in.

There was a general happy murmur that went up from the gathered quilters and Beatrice turned to see Piper coming in with a diaper bag and Will. Beatrice gave her a smile and a wave before Piper was engulfed by Village Quilters. Miss Sissy had even abandoned her plate of food to come over to cuddle Will. Beatrice had wondered if Piper was going to be able to make it, but she'd hoped she could.

After Will had given big smiles to everyone and shown off his new tooth that had miraculously sprung from his gums apparently overnight, Piper settled next to Beatrice on the big, cushy brown sofa.

Beatrice said wryly, "I'll get you a plate of food, but you're going to have to save my spot or else somebody will try to take it." She looked over at Miss Sissy in the armchair directly across from them. She had a feeling the spry old woman would quickly usurp her if she moved an inch.

"I actually ate right before coming over," said Piper with a grin. "So you don't have to worry about fighting over your place. I totally forgot we were meeting at Meadow's or I'd have come over hungry. I was more focused on feeding this little guy."

They looked down at Will and he gave them a gummy grin, the one white tooth sparkling in the bright sunshine coming down from Meadow's skylights in the barn ceiling.

"Where did that tooth come from?" asked Beatrice in a teasing tone. "I swear there was absolutely no evidence of it when I was babysitting him."

"He wasn't drooling all over the place and sticking toys or his entire fist in his mouth?" asked Piper with a smile.

"He certainly was not. Will's face was all neat and tidy and he wasn't sticking anything whatsoever in his mouth."

Piper said, "Maybe the tooth fairy took on a reverse role and *gave* Will a tooth instead of taking one away."

"Does that mean you owe *her* money?" asked Beatrice. "Since she brought a tooth instead of taking one?"

"Probably. We can add her to our long list of creditors," said Piper with a sigh. "Who knew babies were so expensive?"

Will gave her a snuggle as if apologizing and Piper nuzzled the soft hair on the top of his head. "And worth every penny," she admitted.

Beatrice finished her food and then said, "Be prepared for some lightning-fast action from Miss Sissy. I've got to get a refill of tea."

Sure enough, as soon as Beatrice had just barely stood up, Miss Sissy somehow slid herself behind her and plopped down heavily next to Piper on the sofa, reaching peremptorily for the baby.

Beatrice rolled her eyes at Piper, but Piper's eyes just twinkled as she handed Will over to Miss Sissy. Luckily, Will never seemed to feel any sense of separation anxiety from his mother and was contentedly fingering the lace on the end of the old woman's sleeve.

"See you got your place stolen," said Meadow, chortling. "Miss Sissy is a sly one."

"Well, what can you do?" said Beatrice with a shrug. "I think Will gets as much out of it as she does. He seems very fond of Miss Sissy."

"Does she sing to him? I know he loves singing. I hear Miss Sissy has a fantastic voice and is being considered for the church choir," said Meadow. "Who would've thought it? I thought Miss Sissy would have a voice like a croaking frog."

"Let me guess where you heard this rumor," said Beatrice.

Meadow frowned. "Why? Do you think Miss Sissy *can't* sing?"

"I strongly suspect Miss Sissy has no musical ability whatsoever. I also deduce that you heard she could from Dora Tucker."

"How on earth did you know that?" asked Meadow.

"Because she's determined to set Miss Sissy up with an audition with the choir director to get her more involved. She seems like she's been at loose ends lately and Dora thought that might be a good way to take up some of her time."

A few minutes later, Meadow called the meeting to order by ringing an old dinner bell. To Beatrice, she seemed rather obviously eager to get Dora out of her home as expeditiously as possible. "We have a special guest here today, so we'll delay the minutes of the last meeting and our usual business until after Dora has the chance to speak with us." She gave Dora a tight smile. "The floor is yours."

Chapter Twelve

Dora stood up and beamed at everyone as if they were about to be delighted with what everything she had to say. "Thanks for having me today. Meadow, I love your home."

Meadow's tight smile turned into a genuine one for a few seconds before tightening up again.

Dora said, "I'm *soo* excited about the upcoming show and I think y'all will be, too. First up we have a few changes just to keep our guests at the show interested in what we do. Sometimes it's good to switch things up to keep it all fresh and exciting—not just for the attendees of the show, but for the quilters, too."

Meadow started glowering.

"So we decided on a few marvelous changes."

Beatrice winced at the 'we.'

"One of the different approaches we're trying is to offer more substantive food to our quilt show guests this year. Instead of cakes, we're going to be offering a real lunch—sandwiches and chips. At first, I'd considered asking a local restaurant if they wanted to be a vendor for the event, but then I figured if we made the food ourselves that we could keep the profits.

We'll need volunteers to staff the food tables and I've brought a signup sheet for that. The Cut-Ups have already signed up for some of the shifts so if the Village Quilters could fill in for the rest of the slots, that would be great."

Beatrice glanced over at June Bug to see if she was miffed at all that her wonderful cakes were being passed over for basic sandwiches and chips, but as usual, the little woman looked serene: calm and accepting with not a trace of irritation showing as she attentively listened to Dora.

Dora continued. "This also means that we all need to chip in with different types of sandwiches. There's lots of ways to make sandwiches more interesting for our guests. We can use different types of breads, homemade breads, different condiments, different toppings."

Beatrice cleared her throat. "And we'll obviously need a way to keep the sandwiches cool because they'll have meats on them."

Dora gave her an annoyed look at the interruption. "Yes, of course. Anyway, I've also brought a signup sheet so everyone can list the sandwich they're choosing and the chips they're bringing. We'll also have soft drinks and lemonade for sale."

The Village Quilters all looked slightly stunned. This was already quite a bit of change from their usual quilt shows and quite a bit more volunteering of their time than they were used to.

Dora gave them a beatific smile, sharp teeth gleaming. "And now for a truly exciting announcement. My nephew's band has agreed to play during the quilt show. They're wonderful and young and my hope is that they'll help to introduce and entice an entirely different crowd to our show. Perhaps we can even interest some younger folks in quilting while they're there. Their band, Pixie Tribute, will be advertising their appearance on lamp posts around town and on their social media channels. I'm sure they'll have wonderful turnout."

Now there was a buzz in the room as the guild members murmured about this to others and Meadow looked increasingly unhappy.

Meadow said, "But the band is playing something sort of quiet, aren't they? So people can talk. Because everyone does love the chance to talk about their quilts or to catch up with others."

Beatrice cleared her throat. "I think what Dora and I discussed was for the band to be playing folk or jazz music."

Dora's mouth pulled down in dissatisfaction. "We did talk about that, yes. But the problem with that approach is we might not get the traffic from the young people. That occurred to me after we spoke, Beatrice."

Meadow said sweetly, "But if the young people are true friends of the band members, they'll want to hear them no matter what they're playing, just to support them. Right?"

Dora's eyes narrowed but she acquiesced, "I suppose that's right." She gave a bright smile and looked around at everyone in the room. "Anyway, it was a pleasure to visit the Village Quilters today and I'm really looking forward to the show. Beatrice, if you'll collect the signup sheets before you leave Meadow's house and hand them to me later, that would be great. Good to see everyone!" And she quickly made an exit.

After she left, it took a few minutes for everyone to settle down. Posy was concerned about making sure the food they brought to the show was properly chilled. She also brought up that some of the sandwiches might need to be served warm and perhaps they'd need a small microwave there, which meant they'd need to set up the refreshments table near an outlet or bring a long extension cord. Savannah worried about young people driving to the show and the possibility of senior drivers and teen drivers bumping into each other in the narrow aisles of the parking lot outside the community center. Georgia just looked fretful. Meadow continued to glower.

Finally, Beatrice stood up to speak. "I know this is a lot of change to adapt to right now. Believe me, I did try to get some concessions from Dora, but you know how determined she can be."

Meadow muttered something under her breath.

"So let's be practical about this," said Beatrice. "Dora is genuinely trying to do something to attract higher attendance to the show. Her heart is in the right place. The proceeds from the show are going to both our guilds and to the charities of our choice so it's in our best interest to try new things and engage the community a bit more. I wasn't excited about the changes either, but we could give them a go and see how it all works out. If it's a total disaster, we don't have to try it ever again. Or, if it's really a pain in terms of planning, execution, and cleanup, we can go back to the drawing board for next time. All things considered, it's not the end of the world, is it?"

Meadow's expression indicated that she certainly thought it might be, but she surprisingly kept her mouth tightly closed.

Posy said, "Excellent points, Beatrice, and we all appreciate you and the time you and Dora have spent planning the event. I know it will end up being a day we're proud of."

Beatrice was less-certain of this, but smiled at everyone as they appeared to look more cheerful about the quilt show.

The meeting proceeded according to the usual agenda. Beatrice's favorite time was at the end when everyone shared what they were working on. Her friends' creative work never ceased to inspire her. She marveled over Posy's elaborate kaleidoscope pattern quilt with vibrant octagon flowers in shades of pink and blue and Meadow's lovely traditional log cabin quilt. She showed off her own small projects and mentioned how many of her scraps she'd been able to eliminate in the process.

After the meeting wrapped up, Beatrice chatted for a few more minutes before heading back home. She had plenty to do before going to Posy's that night for the movie. Plus, she wanted to make sure Wyatt had something to eat for supper since he'd been kind enough to plan and pick up their meals lately.

Noo-noo looked hopefully at her when she walked in the house, so she quickly took him for a short walk down the street and then fed him. Then she took inventory of the pantry and fridge and made a face. It was starting to look like either grilled cheese sandwiches, black bean quesadillas with a skimpy amount of cheese, or breakfast food.

She decided to go with breakfast food and was just finishing up the eggs and cheese grits when Wyatt came in and gave her a hug.

"How did the guild meeting go? Was there a showdown between Meadow and Dora?" he asked as she handed him a full plate of food.

"I've come to the conclusion that there's really no way to have a showdown with Dora. She somehow acts like we're all on the same page, even when we're not. It was fine—I managed to talk everyone off the cliff after Dora left and Meadow managed to keep a lid on her emotions somehow. How were things at work?"

Wyatt washed down his grits with his glass of milk. "It was all good. I've been asked by Petunia's family to officiate at her funeral in a couple of days. They thought it was best to have her service down here instead of bringing her back to her hometown for interment." His face was solemn.

"How were they?"

He shook his head. "Devastated, of course. They never expected to lose Petunia this young, especially in such a violent way. They seemed so overwhelmed that I offered to handle all of the service details for them so they could just work with the mortician."

Beatrice said, "That must be so hard on them, especially being so far away." They ate quietly for a few minutes and then she said, "Oh, by the way, I'm heading over to Posy's house in a little while. Cork is out of town and she's sort of been at loose ends. More than loose ends, actually—she's been anxious in the evenings being alone after these murders. Savannah, Georgia, and I are heading over to eat with her and watch *The Wizard of Oz*."

Wyatt grinned at her. "That sounds like a very nostalgic evening."

"For some of us! But can you believe Savannah has never watched it? We immediately chose it after she told us. I thought watching that film was practically required of every child."

He said, "I bet she'll love it. And that Posy will love having y'all there to keep her company so she doesn't have to spend the evening alone again."

"What are you and Noo-noo going to do while I'm gone?" asked Beatrice in a teasing voice.

"Something really exciting," said Wyatt with a grin. "At least, for Noo-noo and me."

"What's that?"

"Doze off in front of Jeopardy and Wheel of Fortune."

Noo-noo grinned in agreement.

Later, over at Posy's, Beatrice walked in to the second feast of the day, considering Meadow had already fed her handsomely earlier. Posy had gone all out for them—you could tell she was excited to have them over. She'd served the food buffet-style and they sat out on her screen porch around a big table with their food and glasses of wine. She had some beautiful folk music similar to what she played at the store piped in through a speaker on the porch. They ate and drank and watched the birds come in for their evening meals and go back and forth from the beautiful birdhouses to the feeders. There were cardinals and bluebirds, Carolina wrens, and chickadees.

When the friends were finished eating, they helped Posy clear away the dishes and put away the rest of the food. Then Posy set up the movie in her living room. There was a soft quilt on the back of each chair and sofa and Posy invited them to make themselves comfy to watch the film. Beatrice plopped down on the sofa and groaned. "I can't believe I ate so much lasagna, but it was so good I couldn't seem to stop myself. I may have to pull a Tums out of my purse."

Posy beamed at her. "Isn't that lasagna wonderful? It's my favorite Italian place. And lasagna was their special tonight, so I got lots of it."

Georgia settled into a chair near the television and Savannah sat down next to Beatrice. The doorbell rang and Posy jumped a little before putting her hand to her chest with a rueful chuckle. "You see? I'm just a nervous mess. It's a good thing y'all are here. I'm sure this must be Meadow and Miss Sissy—I asked them to come, and Meadow said she'd bring Miss Sissy over. She couldn't make it for supper, but she was available to watch the movie."

It was indeed Meadow, who came in with a cheery smile, her long, gray braid swinging from side to side as she strode in and hugged everyone. "Hi, everybody!" she sang out. She looked a little like she might be a character in *The Wizard of Oz* herself with her red shoes and her emerald-colored long dress.

Miss Sissy looked grouchy, especially since Meadow had taken a while to arrive and they'd missed the food (even though Meadow had given her fried chicken leftovers from the guild meeting for supper). Posy jumped up and hurried to the kitchen and handed Miss Sissy a large bowl of popcorn. "Miss Sissy, I made this one especially for you."

Miss Sissy managed a smile, a rare expression for her. Posy looked around. "Does anyone else want popcorn with the movie?"

Beatrice groaned again at the mention of food. "Still stuffed Posy, thanks." Actually, she was starting to worry that she might end up falling asleep because she was so full. It didn't help that Maisie, home from the quilt shop with Posy, immediately curled up in a ball of fluff in Beatrice's lap and happily nodded off.

Once the film started, though, Beatrice woke right up, feeling the same sense of delight she had in the past. Her lips twitched up in a smile at the scene where Miss Gulch took off with Toto on her bike since Savannah, in appearance at least, had always reminded her of Miss Gulch and the fact that Savannah took a bicycle everywhere helped support that association. And she loved the part where the movie turned from the black-and-white Kansas scenes to the glorious Technicolor of Oz.

Miss Sissy's eyes were wide and she muttered to herself throughout. "Have you seen the movie before?" Posy asked her. Miss Sissy didn't even spare her a glance, instead saying, "Hush!" The old woman did, oddly, seem very suspicious over Glinda, the Good Witch of the North. Perhaps it had something to do with her arrival in a pink bubble.

Meadow shrieked when the flying monkeys swooped in, which scared them all, even more than the monkeys themselves. She put her hands over her mouth and gave a muffled, "Sorry!"

And Savannah seemed completely enthralled by the characters, the songs, and the story itself. Beatrice saw her wipe a tear away when Dorothy had to say goodbye to her friends to return to Kansas.

When the movie was over, Posy gave them all a warm smile. "I'm so glad you were all here tonight. It was a movie about friendship and you're all the best friends anyone could have."

Meadow asked Savannah, "Did you like the movie? What am I saying? *Everyone* likes *The Wizard of Oz*!"

Savannah nodded. "Every minute. The Cowardly Lion was my favorite, especially when he went to the beauty parlor and got his mane curled. It was scarier than I thought, too, which was fine because I like scary movies. Somehow I'd thought it was all going to be just songs."

"There are definitely some scary parts," said Beatrice.

"Those monkeys!" said Meadow.

"And the hourglass counting down Dorothy's last minutes. And the Wicked Witch melting into a puddle," said Posy.

They chatted for a couple more minutes before Miss Sissy started sleepily and noisily yawning, which quickly became contagious. The group took their leave, Savannah humming "Somewhere Over the Rainbow" as she left.

Chapter Thirteen

The next couple of days passed quietly until the morning of Petunia's funeral. Wyatt had arranged a small graveside service, chosen scripture and music, and invited a soloist from the church choir. The church ladies were in charge of a reception at the church fellowship hall. Wyatt and Beatrice left early to make sure the funeral home had set everything up. Petunia's parents were there early, too, looking pale and pinched at the service of their daughter that they never thought they'd have. It made Beatrice sad to see how young Petunia's parents were . . . they must be around fifty . . . and how horribly shocked they must be to be at their daughter's funeral service.

Her mother quietly gave Wyatt a hug and said somberly, "Thank you. Thank you for setting up the details of the service for us. And thanks so much to the church members for making Petunia feel a part of the church when she was so new in town."

He hugged her back and said, "We're all so sorry about Petunia. I was happy to do what I could. As I mentioned to you earlier, the church will be hosting a reception in our fellowship hall after the service."

Petunia's father and mother nodded and retreated to sit quietly under the funeral home's tent, near their daughter's coffin.

Wyatt spoke quietly with the funeral home director and the soloist while Beatrice walked away to sit on a bench not far away. After ten or fifteen minutes, the mourners started arriving. Because it was a Saturday, it looked like most of the teachers from the school were there, Sterling Wade and Fletcher King among them. And there were also quite a few young children who must have been Petunia's students. It must have been such a terrible blow for children that age and difficult for the school and the kids' parents to try and explain what had happened.

Sterling looked grim and seemed to be blinking a lot to try and keep his emotions at bay. Fletcher simply looked completely exhausted as he probably was, trying to figure out what his next steps were, plus planning a funeral service for his wife. Ramsay was there and seemed to be keeping an eye on the different attendees—in particular, it appeared, Dora Tucker. If Dora noticed, she was just as calm and confident as usual. She gave Beatrice a small wave from across the crowd.

The service began with Wyatt calling for prayer. Afterward, a soloist from the church choir sang the Lord's prayer. She did a beautiful job and Beatrice saw several people dabbing their eyes. Fletcher seemed overcome by emotion and tried to slip quietly away without attracting attention from the service. This attempt fell short when Sterling clumsily approached him, apparently offering to drive him home since Fletcher was teared up. Fletcher waved him angrily away, nearly slugging Sterling in the process. Other mourners were watching the exchange, but pretending not to since the service was still ongoing.

Sterling slowly returned to his spot where he stood quietly for the remainder of the service. The funeral itself was over just twenty minutes later and everyone headed to the church for the reception.

The church ladies, dressed in somber shades of their Sunday best, including Elspeth, had everything completely organized in the church hall. There was a long line of what looked to be delicious Southern cooking in chaffing dishes on long tables covered with a plum-colored tablecloth. The ladies doled out fried chicken, ham biscuits, macaroni and cheese, broccoli casserole, and corn pudding with long-handled serving spoons.

Beatrice went through the buffet line a couple of people behind Sterling. He pleasantly attempted to ask Elspeth how she was doing but Elspeth crossly barked at him to keep moving. Sterling jumped and quickly obeyed, scurrying through the buffet line as fast as he could. When he and Beatrice had made it out of the food line, she caught up with him.

"Elspeth didn't mean anything by that," she said wryly. "The church ladies just like things done a particular way, especially at funeral receptions."

"They like things done like clockwork?" he asked with a twisted smile.

"Exactly." Beatrice watched curiously as he turned even paler than usual and fumbled with his plate. Surely he wasn't about to clumsily drop it on the floor after all the trouble he'd had getting it. She turned to see what he was staring at and saw Ramsay frowning at him from across the room.

Sterling nervously leaned toward Beatrice. "Do you think Ramsay seems suspicious of me? I feel like he keeps staring at me. He did at the funeral service, too."

Beatrice said lightly, "Oh, it's probably just that Ramsay is wishing he was somewhere else . . . reading *Walden* for the hundredth time or penning a short story. Policing isn't his favorite activity."

Sterling gave her a grateful look. "Thanks. You're right; I have no idea what Ramsay is thinking. It's just making me really anxious. I have my career to think of." He laughed dryly. "Maybe it's not the world's top fast-track career, but it's mine and I love it. I'm sure Wyatt feels like he had a calling to the ministry?"

Beatrice nodded and Sterling continued eagerly, "That's precisely how I feel about education. I have only one gift and it's teaching. And parents have entrusted their children to me and I don't want them worried I'm involved in something untoward."

Beatrice had never thought to hear murder termed *untoward*, but she nodded again.

"And now there's been a second death. And another one connected to the school—a spouse of a teacher. I just can't believe it about Edie." He looked down at his plate, which he'd only picked at. "I was just trying to help Fletcher out at the funeral, you know. He didn't look as if he should be driving home in the state he was in. I could understand him being upset, especially with Edie just having died on top of Petunia's death. But he definitely didn't want any help." Sterling gave a short laugh.

Beatrice said, "I'm sure he was gruff because he was just overwhelmed. It's been an incredibly difficult last week for him. He didn't mean anything by it." She couldn't help but think

Fletcher wouldn't have been *quite* as abrupt with someone else, however. He really didn't seem to like Sterling at all.

"Maybe he just feels upset," agreed Sterling.

"Because his wife passed."

"Because they were arguing," said Sterling.

Beatrice frowned. "Were they?"

"The two of them hadn't been getting along well for a while now." He gave that short laugh again. "It's not like Fletcher confided in me, believe me. Everybody could tell. I've heard Fletcher arguing with Edie on the phone quite a few times lately."

"Arguing about what?"

He shrugged. "I was just walking past him in the hall or walking past the gym after school ended the different times I overheard him. I figured they were just going through a rough spot because of moving and all and the stress they were going through with that. Isn't that what they say? That moving is one of the most stressful life experiences you can have?"

Beatrice said, "I know I found it so. I still have a bunch of boxes in my attic that I never unpacked from my move from Atlanta here. I couldn't bear to unpack another box and just abruptly quit. Now I need to just go ahead and give the things away without even looking in the boxes because obviously the items in there aren't remotely important."

Sterling looked thoughtfully at her. "Remind me again what you did in Atlanta when you lived there?"

"I was an art museum curator. It was a museum that primarily focused on folk art and Southern art."

Sterling's eyes lit up. "That's fantastic!"

Beatrice gave him a doubtful look. "Well, I thought it was interesting, but most folks don't give me the enthusiastic response you just did."

"Oh, I was just thinking how marvelous it would be if you would come speak with my class for career day. It's in a few weeks and I can email you with more information."

He looked so excited that she felt she needed to tamp down his enthusiasm just a bit. Perhaps inject a little realism. "Do you think elementary age children would be interested in art museum curation?"

"Definitely! Maybe you could focus on some of the art you saw day in and day out. You could bring in a PowerPoint presentation, for instance."

Beatrice began feeling alarmed. This was sounding like a whole bunch of extra work for someone who was already co-chairing a quilt show, even if Dora hadn't allowed her to do much work for it.

Sterling could apparently see her reluctance because he hastily added, "Or you could just come in and talk. It would only be for ten minutes and then the kids could ask you some questions. It's always fun because you never know what the students are going to say."

Beatrice took a steadying breath and smiled pleasantly. "That would be lovely. Just let me know when and I'll put it on my calendar."

"Piper might enjoy being in there to hear you, too. I'll ask her when I see her," said Sterling.

"Great." Beatrice looked across the dining hall and saw Wyatt with Petunia's family.

Sterling said perceptively, "You probably need to be doing some minister's wife stuff, don't you? I won't hold you up any longer. See you soon."

Beatrice, still holding the plate of food, headed in Wyatt's direction. She was hijacked, however, by Dora Tucker, who grabbed her by the arm.

"Here, why don't we sit together and eat?" she asked. Without waiting for an answer, she steered Beatrice to a nearby table where she plopped down.

Beatrice frowned at her. "I was about to join Wyatt and Petunia's family."

Dora snorted. "With that heaping plate of food? You wouldn't have been able to eat a single bite. Just sit for a minute, talk with me, and then you can head over and speak with the family."

Beatrice suspected this was yet another point Dora was unwilling to let her win. She sat down and stared at Dora somewhat coolly as she ate her food.

"You'll like Petunia's family," said Dora with the tone of someone who'd already crossed that bridge. "I've been helping them go through Petunia's things."

"That's nice of you," said Beatrice stiffly, still aggravated from being waylaid.

Dora shrugged. "It's the hardest thing, isn't it? There's something about the process that feels a little sacrilegious to a family—giving away the loved one's personal things. Of course, I felt sad too but I was able to put that aside and be ruthless with the things. The last thing her mother and father needed was to go back to Iowa with a bunch of stuff. They looked so relieved once we had things sorted into giveaway, trash, and keep piles." She rummaged in her large purse. "Changing tack for a minute, another reason I wanted to speak with you was to give you these."

Dora pulled a bunch of quilt show flyers, bound together with rubber bands, from her purse and handed them to Beatrice.

"I know this isn't the place to be promoting the show," said Dora carelessly, "so just stick them in your purse."

Beatrice's purse wasn't that large. She pressed her lips together tightly in irritation. She'd have to put them in the car since she certainly wasn't going to walk around a funeral reception advertising a quilt show.

"Do you have the signup sheets with you?" asked Dora briskly, an expectant look on her face.

"Are you serious?" asked Beatrice.

This time, Dora had the grace to look slightly ashamed of herself. "You're right, sorry," she said. The words grated out as if Dora didn't have the opportunity to apologize for herself often. Dora sighed. "Sorry," she repeated again, this time sounding more genuine. "You know, I think Petunia's death has affected me more than I want to admit. I've been trying to keep busy so I don't have to think about it. She and I did spend a good deal of time together what with church and being neighbors."

Beatrice nodded. "And it's tough to think about someone being taken so young." She paused and looked at Dora. "And it's hard when sometimes our last interactions with someone were less-than-pleasant, too."

Dora's eyes narrowed. "I can tell somebody's been running their mouth. I can't say I'm too surprised, since Dappled Hills is a veritable hotbed of gossip. Who was it?"

Beatrice had no intention of ratting out Elspeth. "Sorry, I don't remember. One speaks to so many people, you know."

Dora looked irritated. "People in this town are so annoying. Anyway, whoever it is, they're wrong. Not about the argument, which did happen, although it certainly wasn't the last time I saw Petunia. It was a week or more ago. And they're wrong if they think I didn't put things right with Petunia. I'm not the sort to let things go or to let bad feelings fester."

Beatrice silently agreed with her. She certainly *didn't* seem the type. "What was the argument about?"

Dora didn't seem to be surprised by the rather nosy question, possibly because she was fairly nosy herself. "It wasn't about anything, really. It was silly; it was one of those things that I'd let simmer for too long until I blew up." She clicked her tongue, looking irritated with herself. "That's not the sort of thing I usually do. I'd rather address problems I have with people immediately." She gazed at Beatrice as if she might have one or two problems with her right now that needed addressing.

Beatrice gave her what she hoped was a disarming smile. "So, just church stuff, I'm guessing?"

"A bit. You know how I'd been helping to get Petunia involved at the church and introducing her to folks. Petunia started just stepping out of line a bit and started taking over things that were part of *my* provenance."

Beatrice could only imagine. Dora had felt that Petunia was stepping on her toes. Dora liked to be in charge.

"Anyway, my conscience is clear on that front. Like I said, I swallowed my pride and apologized for snapping at her and I'm awfully glad I did. That was at least a week or more before poor Petunia died. And now, here we are with *another* mysterious death." She shook her head and pursed her lips as if Edie had had terrible taste and timing to die in such a fashion and at such a time.

Beatrice would have responded, but her mouth was full of food. She nodded silently. She needed to work her way through the plate of food quickly so she could have an excuse to get away from the table and over to Wyatt.

Dora continued, "Did I hear you found Edie?"

Beatrice swallowed and then washed the food down with some sweet tea. "Unfortunately, so."

"What happened?" asked Dora. "There hasn't been a lot of information out there."

Beatrice gave her a brief recounting while Dora nodded briskly and finished off her food. Beatrice wasn't sure how Dora had made an entire plate of food disappear since she'd been running her mouth, but Dora was apparently as efficient with her eating as she was with everything else.

When Beatrice finished talking, Dora said, "That's just awful. And to think I was at home quilting when Edie was in need." She clicked her tongue and looked annoyed as if no murder should have happened on *her* watch. She frowned at Beatrice. "Aren't you Fletcher and Edie's neighbor?" There was a slight edge to her voice as if Beatrice had been most careless to allow a murder to happen on her street.

Beatrice polished off her food before replying. "I am. And we'd just seen Edie not long before. As I said, it was a terrible thing."

"Shocking," agreed Dora. She reached out and tapped Beatrice on the arm as if Beatrice's attention was starting to wander. "Do you know what you need to do?"

Beatrice didn't, but she was certain Dora was going to tell her.

"You need to organize a neighborhood watch on your street. We have regular meetings and we communicate on social media with each other. I'm the leader of our group."

Beatrice had no doubt of that.

Dora added, "We do a lot of helpful things, not just limited to community safety. We organize trash pickups for our area, for example. You should consider it."

Beatrice said, "Maybe. But we do have the advantage of having the town's police chief living on our street."

Dora was unimpressed with this fact. "And how often is Ramsay at home?"

"When there's a murder case open? Not very often," admitted Beatrice.

"That's exactly what I'm talking about," said Dora in the satisfied tone of one who has won an argument. She tapped Beatrice on the arm again as her gaze strayed toward Wyatt. "There's one other thing I wanted to bring up with you that's critical. Elspeth. Have you noticed that her memory appears to be slipping?"

Beatrice pulled her attention back to Dora with effort. "I haven't myself, no. But I've heard others mention it."

Dora bobbed her head emphatically. "Exactly. People are talking about it. I feel like poor Elspeth might be declining a little. I'd like her daughter's contact information so I can catch her up to speed."

Finally, Beatrice thought, she was one step ahead of Dora. "Actually, Wyatt just did that. Her daughter seemed to take it seriously and will be down here soon."

"Excellent," said Dora shortly in the manner of one who has just ticked something off an extensive mental list. She glanced across the room and apparently spotted someone else she wanted to speak with, or, as Beatrice considered it, harass. "I've got to run, Beatrice. It was good talking to you. Do send me those signup sheets, all right? They're *very* important."

Beatrice felt a sense of relief as Dora disappeared. She stood up and, after putting the flyers in her car, finally headed over to join Wyatt and Petunia's family for the remainder of the reception.

Chapter Fourteen

The rest of the week passed in a sort of blur. Beatrice watched Will on her assigned days and loved spending time with him. Wyatt and she had quiet nights at home with Beatrice quilting and Wyatt reading. And there were, unsurprisingly, the requisite meetings with Dora for the upcoming show. Then there was the setup day the day before.

Beatrice picked up Miss Sissy to take her over to the community center to get the venue setup for the show. The old woman was even more taciturn than usual, giving short, barking replies to any general question Beatrice had. So Beatrice ended up running a vague monologue over the different areas that needed setting-up for the show. At least, she did until Miss Sissy looked balefully at her with an expression that said she knew much better than Beatrice did the ins and outs of setting up a quilt show.

When they walked in, earlier than the scheduled time, Beatrice was somehow not at all surprised to see that Dora was already there. What was more, it seemed Dora had likely been there for a long time. She'd already managed to bring back in the community center's janitorial staff and was showing them how their cleaning efforts after the last event were not quite up to par with her expectations. She was pointing to grimy baseboards as Beatrice and Miss Sissy came in. When she finally spotted them, she headed toward the two women as the janitorial staff looked relieved.

Dora beamed at Miss Sissy. "I am *so* glad you're on our team today. I have a list of things that need to be done. Let me show you how I want the admissions table set up." And she swept the old woman away.

Beatrice, without an assignment, occupied herself by doing the things she knew needed to be done—getting the folding tables out for the refreshments. But apparently, even that wasn't the right thing to have done as Dora trotted back over and said, "Beatrice, please, let's wait for the custodians to vacuum this room again. It really needs it."

Instead, Dora had them both putting out signs she'd made for parking, admissions, and vendor tables. As they worked, she said under her breath, "I'm glad you recruited Miss Sissy into the quilt show backstage work. I did end up taking her over for an audition at the church yesterday for choir." Dora pressed her lips together in displeasure.

Beatrice said mildly, "It didn't go well?"

"It didn't. But that was hardly Miss Sissy's fault. I thought the choir director should have given her more of a chance. After all, God likes hearing *all* voices raised in praise."

"But the choir director didn't agree?" asked Beatrice.

Dora's tone was waspish. "She did not. She said Miss Sissy's singing was like crusty yodeling."

Beatrice managed to hold back her chuckle. She hadn't been able to imagine Miss Sissy with a melodious voice and was glad to some degree to have her opinion upheld by an expert. "Well, there are other ways to keep Miss Sissy involved. Quilting is a natural fit and we're always planning something. You were right to want to keep her more involved. It's not good to be too isolated."

They were interrupted from speaking any more about it by a group of quilters and their husbands coming in with quilts. In only a few hours, the place was transformed and Beatrice finally started looking forward to the event the next day.

The next morning, Beatrice donned khaki slacks and a drapey white blouse. She combed her white-platinum bob into order and took a few deep, centering breaths. It would all go well. Change could be good.

Wyatt came into the kitchen and laughed. "We look like twins," he said with his eyes crinkling. He was wearing khakis and a button-down white top.

Beatrice snorted. "I guess married people really *do* start to look like each other." She looked at him thoughtfully over her cereal bowl. "You're not thinking of spending all day out there, are you?"

"I thought I would. Maybe I could give you a hand."

Beatrice said, "That's really sweet of you, but you don't have to. You've already spent a lot of time helping me set up. Plus, there will be changes this year, like I was telling you."

Wyatt nodded, picking up his juice glass. "Right—the live band."

"Not only that, but June Bug won't have her cakes this year."

Wyatt's face fell comically and Beatrice held back a laugh.

"No cake?" he asked slowly in a sad voice.

"No. We're selling sandwiches and chips."

Wyatt tried to be encouraging about this surprising change. "Well, that will be filling, at least. Not that June Bug's cakes weren't filling."

Beatrice said, "And I think it will be loud in there with the band playing. There seemed to be a lot of speakers they were setting up yesterday. I'm not sure anyone will be able to hear themselves talk and I know you usually enjoy catching up with people at the show."

Wyatt was looking far less enthusiastic now, but still tried to be supportive. "It'll be all right, I'm sure."

"Why don't we take two cars? That way I won't feel like I'm keeping you stuck there if it all starts going downhill."

Wyatt's eyes twinkled. "Downhill? You're making it sound like some sort of raucous event instead of a multi-guild quilt show serving sandwiches and lemonade."

"We might be surprised how raucous it does get," said Beatrice dryly. "Meadow might have a hissy fit."

So they did end up taking a couple of cars. Wyatt helped bring in the food and beverages Beatrice had signed up for.

The band was already tuning up. The young men and young woman all had long hair and baggy clothes. But when Beatrice and Wyatt went over to say hi, they all gave them big smiles, thanked Beatrice for the opportunity, and told her to let them know if they needed to make any changes to their set or anything else.

She left, feeling slightly unsettled, but in a good way. Wyatt grinned at her. "They seem like nice young people. Willing to make concessions."

Beatrice gave a small smile in return. "I'm going to blame Dora for giving me the wrong mental image."

Wyatt chuckled. "Blame Dora?"

"Why not? She's caused a lot of drama so she deserves it. But the way she described the band didn't exactly inspire confidence."

Wyatt asked, "How did she describe it?"

"I think the term was 'nephew's rock band.'"

"Dire, indeed," said Wyatt, repressing another chuckle.

Beatrice gave him a wry look. "Anyway, we'll see how it goes. And the other changes. And now I suppose I need to make myself busy since Dora is buzzing around."

Dora was definitely buzzing. She was flitting from quilt display to quilt display and staring critically at everything with narrowed eyes. She'd arrange the fabrics, run over to the refreshments table, and moved the bags of chips into perfect lines. She had even approached the vendor tables and tried to get them to organize their displays better. Beatrice had to admit though that everything was in place and very organized. It was very possibly the best-run show she'd seen yet.

Beatrice checked in at the food table, which is where Posy had the first shift. "How are things going here?" asked Beatrice with a small grimace. "I saw Dora just light into everyone here."

"Oh, she didn't like the sign we made," said Posy with a smile and a shrug.

"The sign? What on earth is wrong with it?" asked Beatrice, trying to see the "Sandwiches and Beverages" sign through Dora's eyes.

"Not big enough."

Beatrice frowned. "It's on poster board, for heaven's sake."

"Yes, but the *lettering* wasn't big enough. I'm just going to flip it over and make it bigger on the back. Dora brought some magic markers."

"Of course she did," said Beatrice with a sigh.

Posy flipped the poster board around and then gave Beatrice a hopeful smile. "Actually, I recall that you have some of the best handwriting I've ever seen."

"I believe you're misremembering," said Beatrice in a dry voice. "But I can take a stab at it, if you like."

Posy handed her the markers and gave a relieved sigh. "I do really like Dora. She has such wonderful qualities."

"Mmm-hmm," said Beatrice in an unsure tone as she carefully lettered the sign.

"And she certainly spends money at my shop," said Posy, brightening as she recalled some particularly good recent sales.

"I'm sure she does."

"But she's so . . . intense, isn't she?" asked Posy slowly. "Whenever I'm speaking with her, I feel like she's so incredibly focused. She has so much drive, so much energy."

"And she likes things done her way," added Beatrice. "I tried to keep mostly out of her way and let her do what she wanted. Until Meadow objected, anyway."

Cork, Posy's husband, came up to the table. He was bald and as grim as Posy was cheerful. But he was a kind man and a very creative one. His creative outlets were the birdhouses and feeders that populated their yard, and Beatrice's yard, too.

"Talking about that one over there?" he asked gruffly, nodding toward Dora, who appeared to be directing a scowling Miss Sissy how to better collect tickets and give change.

"How could you tell?" asked Beatrice with a smile. She stopped lettering the sign.

Cork gave a chuckle. "She's something else. Bossy. But gets things done. Still, she's got a real temper on her. She really blew up."

Beatrice frowned. "Dora did? When? Not during set-up yesterday, was it?" If there was one thing Beatrice couldn't countenance, it was anybody giving their volunteers a hard time.

He shook his head. "No, no. Not the volunteers. I don't think she'd even go that far because volunteers can just walk away, can't they? No, I mean she blew up at that young teacher. I could see the veins in her throat. Face was bright red."

Posy put her hand in front of her mouth and Beatrice asked intently, "The young teacher? Do you mean Petunia?"

Cork nodded and Beatrice asked, "When was this?"

"The day before I left town. I was opening up the shop for the day and saw Dora cross the street to give Petunia a piece of her mind."

Posy's eyes were wide with concern as she looked at Beatrice. "That must have been the day before . . . it happened."

Beatrice nodded. "And Dora said she'd argued with Petunia a long while before then and they'd made up."

Posy said sadly to Cork, "I didn't even have the chance to tell you since you came back home, but there's been a couple of terrible tragedies since you left. Murders." She grimaced. "I didn't want to worry you while you were away."

Cork's heavy-lidded eyes opened as wide as they could. "You mean Petunia?"

"She was one of the victims," said Beatrice somberly. "Could you hear what the argument was about, Cork?"

He shook his head. "Not really. Something to do with the church, though. Petunia was on some committee that was doing something Dora didn't like? Something like that. I was mostly just trying to get out of their way and get the shop open."

Beatrice said, "Cork, you or Posy need to tell Ramsay about this."

Posy shook her head and lowered her voice to a whisper. "Do you think we should? I just can't imagine Dora killing Petunia. Won't we just get her in trouble if we say anything?"

"If she hasn't done anything, she has nothing to worry about," said Beatrice. She paused. "I bet Ramsay will be here later today to check in. You should tell him. Dora specifically told me that she and Petunia had argued long before she died and that they'd made up. It seems to me like she deliberately concealed that they quarreled the day before Petunia's death."

Posy nodded, looking miserably across the room at Dora who appeared to be checking things off of a legal pad. "All right, Beatrice. You're right—it's something he should know about."

Cork said, "I'll send him a text message. But I know he's busy now, it might be a while before he can get back to me."

Posy turned pink as Dora strode toward them. "Oh no. Here she comes."

"Hi ladies," said Dora briskly. "Can I steal you both away for a minute? I need some help at the door."

An hour later, Beatrice had to admit that the quilt show was going surprisingly well. The band had their speakers turned down low and the singer had a beautiful voice. They'd clearly tried to keep their music mellow and even played a couple of old standards that had the seniors at the show tapping their feet to the beat. The band had apparently really put a call out on social media, too, because there were a lot of younger people in attendance, too and they made for an enthusiastic audience.

Meadow strolled over to Beatrice for their joint shift at the food and beverage table. She sighed and said to Beatrice, "I give up."

"You give up on what?" Beatrice asked vaguely as she studied the list of sandwiches. Her stomach growled to remind her she hadn't had anything to eat for a while.

"I give up on criticizing Dora. It's just so very annoying when she's right." Meadow's lips tightened. Then she grew distracted as she, too, glanced over the sandwich list. "Mercy! These are some fancy sandwiches here. I feel a little guilty just bringing in basic BLTs."

Beatrice gave her a wry look. "Yes, but the difference between your BLTs and anyone else's are that you have home-grown tomatoes in them. And, if I remember, locally-sourced bacon. So your basic sandwich is practically gourmet quality. Whereas my pimento cheese sandwiches are genuinely basic."

"Now, you know I've always liked your pimento cheese! Especially when you make your spicy kind. Is this the spicy kind with the jalapenos?"

Beatrice shook her head sadly. "No, I ran out of time. I just have the regular kind: cheese, mayo, mustard, and pimentos."

"Well, that's just fine, too! We're all doing what we can, aren't we?"

A young woman came up and asked for a lemonade and a roast beef sandwich, which interrupted their conversation for a few minutes. After the young woman left, Beatrice asked in a carefully-casual tone, "Is Ramsay coming here later?"

"Why?" asked Meadow, eyes wide. "Do you know something? You know something, don't you?" She began looking suspiciously around the room as if a murderer were lurking among the quilts, ready to leap out at a moment's notice.

"I don't know anything. But Cork apparently witnessed a big blow-up between Dora and Petunia shortly before Petunia ended up dead. But when I spoke to Dora, she said she and Petunia had patched up a misunderstanding they'd had and it had been long before Petunia's death. I persuaded them that they really needed to say something to Ramsay about it."

Meadow looked stormy. "Dora. I should have known it. And here I was finally coming around to her bossy way of doing things and she's a double-murderer."

"We don't *know* anything. Cork or Posy is merely reporting something Cork saw and heard. Is Ramsay going to be here later?"

"Oh, he'll be here, all right. I made it clear in no uncertain terms that he needed to check in just for five or ten minutes," said Meadow. Her eyes indicated that Ramsay would be in trouble indeed if he didn't show up.

Beatrice said mildly, "Well, he *is* working really hard right now. I'd imagine a murder investigation doesn't leave room for many breaks."

"But he has to eat! And now we have these sandwiches and things, so he might as well come in and grab a sandwich." Meadow glared at the offending sandwiches, although she showed every indication of being very interested in trying one.

Someone else came up for a sandwich and then Meadow said, "All right, I'm caving in. I don't think it's bad to eat during our shift. We'll be advertising how tasty the sandwiches are. I'm happy to make faces showing how much I'm enjoying the food." She pulled out a few dollars and slapped them on the table in front of Beatrice. "I'm going to get myself a Cuban sandwich."

Beatrice paid for one of Meadow's BLTs with the homemade tomatoes. After they took their first bites, they saw Dora from across the room giving them reproachful looks.

"Looks like we've upset Dora," mused Beatrice.

"Oh, it's impossible *not* to upset Dora. She's not the boss of me!" Meadow took another enthusiastic bite of her sandwich.

Wyatt came up to them and gave them a grin. "Sampling the wares?"

"They're some pretty excellent wares," said Meadow. "What'll you have?"

Wyatt carefully studied the menu and said, "Maybe a chicken salad sandwich?"

"Good choice," said Meadow. "Posy brought those in and I know her chicken salad is amazing. She has grapes and almonds in it and always has a little fresh dill."

Wyatt paid for his food and lemonade and joined them for a few minutes, enjoying his sandwich and listening to them while they chatted.

Meadow said, "So Beatrice, get me caught up on what you've found out. I need to know before Ramsay does . . . I like to be one-up on him."

"I'm not sure exactly *what* I've found out except that everyone seemed to have all sorts of tangled-up issues with everyone else," said Beatrice. "Sterling Wade had a crush on Petunia. Fletcher might have been involved with Petunia, himself. Elspeth had an argument with Petunia. Dora did, too."

"And what do any of them have to do with Edie? She wasn't a teacher at the school," said Meadow. "She seems like the real mystery to me. If she wasn't at the school, how did she end up involved in all this?"

Beatrice sighed. "All I'm guessing is that Edie knew something and the murderer needed to silence her. But I don't really have any idea."

Meadow said, "Well, I hope Ramsay can figure this all out soon. He's been a real mess this time. I can tell he's sort of going through the motions and really letting the state police take the lead on a lot of the investigating."

Wyatt gave her a sympathetic look. "I remember you mentioned that Ramsay is interested in retiring. Maybe he's just having a tough time getting motivated?"

Meadow snorted. "The motivation should be easy—ridding our poor town of a murderer! But I think you're right; all Ramsay is thinking of is what *else* he could be doing instead of tracking down a killer. He's been really down in the mouth lately, wishing he could be reading a book or writing some short stories. But it's also been tough on him because he's trying to still be a good partner with the state police. He hasn't been sleeping well because they've called him at all hours. And he's not eating on a regular schedule, either."

"Well, I hope he finds time to stop by and grab a sandwich," said Beatrice. She somehow felt doubtful about this. With so much on Ramsay's mind and so much on his plate, how likely was it that he'd find the time to pop in to a quilt show?

Chapter Fifteen

The show actually went surprisingly well. Although many people bemoaned the lack of June Bug's cake slices, the sandwiches were a hit. And the young band members not only acted extremely professionally, they also continued to bring in a stream of young people as they had a friend post pictures of them playing on social media. Beatrice watched as Meadow and Posy introduced the quilts to a group of interested visitors. It was all turning out very well in the end.

After a while, Beatrice saw Elspeth come in with Sterling Wade. She spotted Beatrice, waved, and they came over.

"Welcome to both of you," said Beatrice with a smile.

Elspeth said, "Oh, I'm excited to be here. I've been meaning to come back to a show for the past couple of years but just haven't managed to make it. I was talking about it at the school with Sterling and he said he'd go with me, so here we are!" Her eyes were bright. She glanced around. "Is Wyatt here?"

Beatrice smiled at the fan-girl attention Wyatt always seemed to get. "I'm afraid he's already left for the day. He was here earlier helping to set up and then he had lunch and headed home."

Elspeth looked disappointed. "Oh, well. I'll see him on Sunday." She glanced at Sterling with a smile. "As you can see, I got Sterling to come. He said he'd never been to a quilt show and I thought that was a pity, especially with all the talent we have here in Dappled Hills."

Sterling said, "I haven't been to one at all, but I've seen the flyers at school. I always love showing the kids in my class different things and I thought I'd take pictures of some of the quilts so they could have a sort of virtual visit. Maybe I can take some short videos, too, of the quilters talking about their designs and how they made the quilts."

"Great idea," said Beatrice. "I bet the students will love seeing all the different kinds of quilts."

Elspeth spotted Meadow and excused herself to hurry over. Beatrice gave Sterling a quick overview of the types of quilts he'd be seeing and the variety of styles and techniques. He nodded and at one point took out his phone to make notes as Beatrice spoke. "Terrible memory," he said wryly. He looked around him. "This is a nice crowd here."

"Yes, we've had especially good turnout today. You know Dora Tucker from church, of course."

"Of course," said Sterling, quirking an eyebrow. "She manages nearly everything there."

"Dora had a lot of ideas that she worked hard to implement to make the quilt show more of a success," said Beatrice. She felt proud of herself for giving Dora credit for the show.

"Well, she certainly did a good job, although that's really no surprise. And it's a nice diversion, with everything that's been going on." A shadow covered Sterling's face at the thought of the recent events. He added, "Have you heard whether Ramsay has made any progress with the cases?"

"I'm sure he has, although I haven't really spoken with him."

Sterling sighed. "I hope he does soon. The more I think about it, the more agitated I feel. Two women who were in the prime of their lives. They didn't deserve this." He paused again and then said in a low voice, "And the more I think about it, the more I feel like I know who's behind these deaths."

Beatrice wrinkled her brow. "Who?"

Sterling spread his hands out before him as if the answer were there right in front of them, very plainly. "Fletcher King. It makes the most sense. He was Edie's spouse and the spouse is always the primary suspect. I know they were arguing, like I mentioned to you before. And he was involved with Petunia."

"Was he?" asked Beatrice, staring at him. She felt a frisson of uneasiness. She thought no one knew about Fletcher and Petunia besides Piper, Beatrice, Ramsay, and Wyatt.

Sterling reddened a little. "He was. Or he was trying to be involved with her, either way. And who had the most opportunity to murder both Petunia and Edie? Fletcher. He was the one who discovered Petunia, but he probably just acted like he'd 'discovered' her because Piper showed up when she did. Easy to discover someone when you've just murdered them." His voice was bitter.

"And Edie? Fletcher was supposed to be at school."

"But was he? He doesn't have a class for the last block of the day—it's his planning period. He could easily have slipped out and murdered his wife and then headed back to the school so everyone could see him leave," said Sterling. He looked sharply at Beatrice. "You look worried."

Beatrice shook her head and gave a short laugh. "Aren't you?" She felt like she was in a cloud.

"Not worried, just mad." He gave her a sharp look again as if worried she needed to sit down. "Look, I'm sorry. Here you're trying to relax and enjoy the quilt show you've been organizing and I'm running my mouth. I'll catch up with Elspeth and take some pictures of quilts." And with that, he hurried off.

Beatrice started another shift, this time helping guests sign in at the door as Miss Sissy went over to man the refreshments table. She only hoped that whoever was working the table with Miss Sissy would make sure she didn't eat all of the merchandise. Then the rest of the afternoon was a blur of activity and prizes. June Bug won in the Large Applique category and Dora won for Computer-Assisted. Miss Sissy proudly accepted a first-place ribbon for a pieced, large quilt. The winners were congratulated and the band played upbeat songs until it was time to start packing things up and taking down the quilts. The vendors put their displays away and into their vehicles. The band beamed at the round of applause they got and then packed up their equipment.

Everyone left with their quilts and then it was just a matter of getting the venue back to normal—taking out trash bags, wiping down the tables and chairs and stacking them up and away. Miss Sissy had helped the entire day and she was starting to look tired.

Beatrice walked over to Meadow. "Why don't you go ahead and get Miss Sissy back home? She's been here for hours, helping out. Dora and I can handle the rest of everything."

"Are you sure?" Meadow's voice was doubtful, but she looked tired herself. "If you really think so, I'll take her home. Then I'll go home myself and plan on telling Ramsay Downey that he forgot something very, very important." Her voice was cross.

"Don't give him too hard of a time. He's probably been out working on these cases all day long and the show was the last thing on his mind."

Meadow grudgingly conceded this. Then she gave Dora a side eye as she busily swept a corner of the venue. "Are you sure you're going to be safe with Dora? Didn't we decide some of her behavior was a little suspect? She might be dangerous."

Beatrice glanced over at Dora. Maybe she *was* dangerous, but she certainly looked completely innocuous at the moment. "I don't think Dora would want to do anything that would make her very successful event look bad. And murdering her quilt show co-chair would definitely qualify as something to make it look bad."

Meadow looked unsure. "All right. I guess you're right. Although I still would feel better if you weren't alone with her."

Beatrice said, "We won't be here long—there isn't that much to clean up. Oh, could you ask Ramsay to give me a call? It doesn't have to be tonight if he's really exhausted. I just wanted to update him."

"Got it," said Meadow. "And Posy or Cork wanted to talk with him too, right? Sounds like he'll have a round of phone calls to make. She found Miss Sissy and they walked out the door together, Miss Sissy looking quite tired but very happy. It must have been rewarding for her to volunteer for the event.

Dora and Beatrice were the last ones left then. Dora was whistling a peppy tune and seemed, to Beatrice's chagrin, to somehow have just as much energy at the end of the day as she'd had in the beginning while Beatrice was starting to drag, especially since it was the second day in a row she'd had a lot of physical activity. Dora appeared to be one of those indefatigable people who just dives into cleaning. With someone like that, it's hard to know how to join in because they seem to be everywhere at once, capably handling the clean-up.

Dora stood still for a moment and surveyed the room, which to Beatrice looked spic-and-span. "I think we're just about done, don't you? I think I missed that area over there with the broom, though, so I'm going to touch it up. Beatrice, could you take this bag of trash out for me?"

Beatrice picked up the bag of paper plates and cups and trudged toward the dumpster outdoors. The parking lot was now basically deserted and the sun was going down. Although she'd had that sandwich earlier, she hadn't had a chance to have anything else to eat—a fact that her stomach growlingly reminded her of. She couldn't wait to get back home, eat something, and then crawl into bed.

She walked toward the dumpster and felt a prickling sensation that told her someone was there. She turned, expecting to see Dora, but was surprised to see Sterling Wade. Beatrice raised her eyebrows. "Sorry, Sterling, the quilt show is over. Were you trying to get more pictures for the kids?"

He said lightly, "Oh, I know it's over—I was driving by on my way to the store and saw you alone out here. Can I give you a hand with the clean-up?"

Something made Beatrice avoid mentioning that Dora was still there to help. She realized Dora had parked at the back of the building to carry in things that morning and her car wasn't visible. "Sure, Sterling, thanks. Do you mind tying off this bag and throwing it in the dumpster for me?"

"Absolutely." He did and then turned with a smile. "I know you're probably fine out here, but with everything going on, it would make me feel better if I gave you a hand while you're cleaning up. Wyatt couldn't be here?"

"He was here for the show setup yesterday and then was here during the show for a couple of hours before I sent him on his way. But I appreciate your help. It has been very odd in Dappled Hills lately. Maybe it will all wrap up soon."

"Maybe so," he said. He gave Beatrice another of those probing looks. "It's all very strange, isn't it? I keep thinking there must be something about these deaths that I'm missing somehow. It wasn't even maybe *planned*. Maybe it was just a crime of opportunity."

Beatrice couldn't see Sterling's face because there was a shadow over it. But there was an earnestness, a persuasiveness in his voice. And all of a sudden she was very aware of the fact that Sterling earlier had mentioned Fletcher and Petunia's relationship. The relationship no one actually knew about. A chill went up her spine and she took a step away from Sterling.

"What do you mean? A crime of opportunity?" asked Beatrice.

"You know. The perpetrator of the murders used whatever was close to hand. The globe. A shovel."

Beatrice froze. No one knew that information. She hadn't told anyone and it wasn't general knowledge. She had to get out of here so she could tell Ramsay.

"Right. You're absolutely right, Sterling," she said hurriedly. She hesitated and said, "I really appreciate your offer of help. I think I've got it from here, though. Lifting that heavy bag into the dumpster was the last big thing. It's really now just a matter of locking up and dropping off the key in the lockbox."

Sterling tilted his head to one side like an inquisitive bird. "You seem really nervous, Beatrice."

She let out a short laugh. "Nervous? No. I'm just very tired, that's all. Thanks again for your help." The last was said in a slightly dismissive tone.

But Sterling was apparently not planning on going anywhere. He pulled a knife out of his pocket. "Let's go inside," he said in a hard voice.

Beatrice backed away from him and he brandished the knife at her. "Back inside!" he barked.

Beatrice stumbled toward the community center in the dark. Suddenly, the door swung abruptly open and Dora stood there, holding a broom. "What in the dickens is going on out here?" she bellowed in her authoritative, outraged voice.

Sterling's jaw dropped. He scrambled backward to get away as Dora repeated her question in an even louder, more strident, voice as if Sterling might have suddenly become deaf.

"Leave me alone," he snarled, making stabbing motions with his knife to discourage them from following him. He dashed toward his car, shoving his hand in his pocket for his keys. He proceeded to drop them and grabbled on the gravel for them as Dora let out a furious roar and charged at him, wielding the broom violently.

Dora swung at him and Sterling dropped the knife and his keys. Beatrice, ducking Dora's wild swings with the broom, grabbed them both as Sterling loped down the street. He ran until Ramsay, belatedly remembering his duty to pop by the quilt show, came right toward him in his police cruiser, before screeching to a stop just a couple of feet away as Sterling froze in his headlights. Ramsay spotted Dora and Beatrice and then turned on his lights and siren.

Sterling pivoted and scampered, half-heartedly, a minute longer in the opposite direction until he came to a stop with his hands in the air. Ramsay hopped out of the police car and ordered Sterling to the ground. He patted him down roughly and then handcuffed him and read him his rights as Dora scathingly reported Sterling's moral shortcomings in a furious tone. Ramsay seated Sterling in the back of the police car, leaving the door open so they could talk with him. "Don't even think about going anywhere," said Ramsay grimly as if reading Sterling's intentions. Dora brandished the broom at Sterling again while Ramsay made a quick call to the state police.

Ramsay put away his phone and then looked grimly at Sterling. "All right, then. Let's have a little chat before the boys with the state police come over. What exactly was going on here? I thought I was heading to a quilt show and instead I come across . . . this."

Sterling was perspiring profusely and his eyes continued to dart from side to side as if looking for a possible avenue for his escape. He pressed his lips tightly together.

Ramsay said, "Okay. So we'll start with Beatrice and Dora. Dora, I believe you were saying something about Beatrice and Sterling and a knife."

Dora narrowed her eyes at Sterling. "Beatrice was out taking the trash to the dumpster. She didn't come back and I wanted to make sure she hadn't had some sort of medical event or something. I opened up the door to check on her and there was Sterling, pushing Beatrice inside and holding a knife."

Sterling said in a low voice, "I didn't even touch her with it."

Beatrice said, "Well, the intent was there."

Ramsay pulled out his tiny notebook and pencil. "You believe he planned on doing you harm."

"No question."

Sterling glared at her.

Ramsay nodded and said, "And what happened beforehand to make him behave this way? Did you find something out?"

Beatrice sighed. "I wish you'd come earlier to the quilt show."

Ramsay grimaced. "Believe me, I wish I had, too. Meadow is really going to let me have it later."

Beatrice continued, "I was going to tell you a couple of things." She glanced at Dora, whose argument with Petunia she'd been planning on informing Ramsay about, and quickly said, "One of them doesn't matter now. But I was also going to tell you that I'd had a conversation with Sterling earlier and he'd mentioned Fletcher and Petunia's relationship. I wasn't aware that anyone else knew about that and I was going to ask you about it. I wondered, if you knew about it, why you didn't mention it to the police or anyone else."

Ramsay raised his eyebrows. "No one did know about it. It sounds like a secret that Fletcher wanted to keep under wraps. How did *you* find out about it, Sterling?"

Sterling shifted his shoulders a little as if trying to make himself more comfortable. "People knew about it," he muttered.

"Nope. People didn't." Ramsay glowered at him.

Sterling said, "Okay, so they kept it under wraps. You can see how wrong that is, can't you?" His face and neck were streaked with red and he spat out, "Fletcher didn't want to do right by Petunia. He wasn't trying to have any kind of future with her."

Beatrice said, "You're the one who wanted a future with Petunia."

Sterling nodded. "Of course. I wanted to do things the right way. But instead, she had this affair with Fletcher."

Ramsay interjected, "So, Sterling, you said something about Fletcher and Petunia and that set off Beatrice's alarm bells—is that right? Then you realized she knew about you and you wanted to shut her up."

Chapter Sixteen

Sterling narrowed his eyes and shook his head, looking at Beatrice. Beatrice took a deep breath and said, "No, that actually happened earlier today. Like I was saying, I wanted to tell you if you came by the show this afternoon. But then a few minutes ago, Sterling drove by and saw me alone outside at the dumpster. He didn't think anyone else was here because Dora parked out back to leave room for other cars in the parking lot. I think he realized I knew something this afternoon and that's why he came back although he said he returned to help me when he saw me with the trash bag."

Sterling shrugged and then winced as his handcuffed arms protested the motion. "I wasn't sure what I'd said, but Beatrice looked worried this afternoon. Not 'tired', like she'd said. I wanted to see what she knew."

Beatrice raised her eyebrows. "He got back on the subject of the murders to find out exactly what I knew, I guess. Then he proceeded to tell me that the crimes were probably not premeditated because the weapons were everyday objects. Then I *knew*. Because you wanted to keep that information quiet, Ramsay, and he shouldn't have known about the globe and the shovel."

Ramsay nodded. "And so you realized, Sterling, that Beatrice knew you killed Petunia and Edie. You decided to shut her up so she wouldn't reveal anything."

Sterling shrugged and winced again.

Dora hissed, "Idiot!"

Ramsay said, "Okay, give me a little overview over what happened with these deaths, Sterling, before the state cops get here. What made you decide to murder Petunia?"

Sterling looked down and mumbled something.

"What's that?" Ramsay put his hand to his ear. "I can't hear what you're saying."

Sterling lifted his head and said angrily, "I saw her that morning with Fletcher. And she'd finally told me she'd meet me for ice cream after work. It was going to be our first date."

Ramsay said, "And you saw red."

Sterling sighed. "I wasn't happy. I'd been talking to Petunia for a while and bringing her little gifts at school: candy, flowers, stuff like that. Emailing her, texting her."

Ramsay lifted an eyebrow. "Clearly not knowing when to give up."

Sterling's eyes narrowed as if still unwilling to really believe that Petunia wasn't interested. "She was coming around. We had a date set up, like I said. Anyway, she'd have definitely been seeing me if she'd had more time. Fletcher was using up all Petunia's free time and he didn't even *care* about her."

Beatrice said, "And you saw her together with Fletcher the morning she died."

Sterling looked down again. "I came in early that morning to talk with Petunia. I guess Fletcher had come in even earlier and I saw through Petunia's classroom window that they were . . . *embracing*." He said the word as if it left a bad taste in his mouth.

Ramsay asked, "Was that the first you realized they were having a relationship?"

Sterling nodded. "I wanted to kill them. Both of them."

Ramsay tilted his head to the side. "But I guess you figured you wouldn't have as much of a chance with the gym teacher."

Sterling shook his head. "He's a pretty big guy. I'm not stupid. But I saw red. Then I saw Fletcher heading out to the door to come out to the parking lot and I stepped off to the side of the building so he couldn't see me. I figured he'd left something in his car and he needed to get it. After he'd gone out, I went inside."

Dora broke in furiously. "And what did that fix, Sterling? Killing Petunia just eased your pride a little, right? What problems did it solve for her?"

Beatrice thought Sterling actually looked a little ashamed of himself. "Like I said, I saw red. I wasn't really thinking much at all. I didn't *plan* on killing her. I was just going to give Petunia a piece of my mind, that's all."

Ramsay said, "But you ended up losing it at some point."

Sterling looked down again. "Yeah. I picked up the globe and hit her over the head with it. Then I had to leave real quick because I thought I could hear Fletcher coming back."

"Which I'm guessing is where Edie comes in," said Beatrice.

Sterling glanced up, anger flushing his cheeks. "Edie did that to herself. I had no plans on getting rid of Edie. She did it to herself."

Dora barked at him, "She *murdered* herself? Don't be an idiot."

Sterling flushed even redder. "I'm not saying she murdered herself. I'm saying that she was the one who set the whole thing in motion. She told me later that Fletcher had apparently left something at home—his phone. He'd called home from the school's phone and she drove over to the school to bring it to him."

Beatrice said, "So when you saw Fletcher heading into the parking lot, he wasn't going to his car—he was going to Edie's car."

"Right. She apparently saw me sneaking around, making sure Fletcher didn't see me when he left the building." He looked irritated with himself. "I didn't hear a car coming into the parking lot because I was so focused on what was going on inside."

Ramsay said in a grave voice, "And when Fletcher found Petunia dead later, Edie put two-and-two together. So what happened then? Did she call you up and tell you what she'd seen? She apparently didn't tell Fletcher what she'd found out because he wasn't targeted."

"Edie said they needed money. She and Fletcher wanted to start a family and wanted Edie to be able to stay home with the baby and stop working in real estate. But Fletcher didn't make a lot off his gym teacher salary. She told me she'd seen what I'd done and she needed me to give her money so she didn't say anything."

"That must have been a shock," said Ramsay dryly.

"It was scary. I left school right after I got the kids to the bus parking lot and headed off to Edie's house before Fletcher left."

"But instead of giving her money, you killed her," said Dora, fairly bristling with fury.

"It was her fault! I never would have laid a finger on her if she hadn't tried to blackmail me. I don't even *have* any money. I couldn't have paid her even if I'd wanted to. But I went over to her house to talk to her. She was outside working in the yard around the side of the house. I was just going to tell her I couldn't afford to be blackmailed and tried to talk some sense into her. But she turned her back on me and said she'd have no choice but to go to the police. There was a shovel nearby so I just picked it up and swung it at her." Sterling said this in a matter-of-fact voice that made a chill go up Beatrice's spine.

"Got it," said Ramsay in a chipped tone. "Okay, I think that's all I need to hear right now." He shut the car door, trapping Sterling inside as the state police drove up.

After speaking to the police officers for a few minutes, Ramsay returned to Beatrice and Dora. Dora was still indignantly fuming over Sterling's many iniquities as Beatrice suddenly felt very weary. Ramsay seemed to notice this because he said, "The state police are going to take Sterling in one of their cars. How about if I take you home, Beatrice? Then Wyatt can drive you out here tomorrow morning to pick up your car. It's been a long day."

It definitely had. And Beatrice's phone chirped at her right that second. She looked at it and said, "It's Wyatt. And suddenly, I don't feel up to really explaining what happened."

"Of course you don't!" said Dora. "This whole thing was completely absurd."

Beatrice had the feeling that, if Dora had been the killer, the entire enterprise would have been run a lot better.

Ramsay nodded. "I'll take you back and fill Wyatt in. Then I'll head home, myself, just to let Meadow know the case is wrapped up before I head back over to speak with the state police. Since the murderer is caught that will be an excellent way to distract Meadow from the fact that I didn't make it over to the quilt show."

Beatrice gave him a grateful look. "That sounds perfect, thanks." She took a step toward the cruiser and then turned to Dora. "Thanks for coming out when you did. And threatening Sterling like that."

Dora gave her a fierce and unexpected hug that knocked Beatrice slightly off-balance. "Of *course* I did. The very *idea* of him behaving that way!"

Dora kept a watchful eye on Beatrice until she'd climbed safely into the passenger side of Ramsay's police car before striding off to her own vehicle. Beatrice sent a quick text to Wyatt to tell him she was on her way home.

Ramsay, perhaps trying to calm Beatrice or perhaps trying to gather information to placate Meadow later, asked how the quilt show had gone, especially after all the changes. Beatrice did find herself relaxing a little as she talked about the day and how well it had gone.

Ramsay pulled into Beatrice's driveway and they walked up to the door, Noo-noo watching them excitedly from the front window. Beatrice fished out her keys from her purse and opened the door. Wyatt stood up with concern as he saw Ramsay there and saw Beatrice's pale features. "Everything all right?"

"Everything is all right now," said Ramsay before launching into a quick explanation of what happened as Beatrice sat on the sofa and snuggled with Noo-noo.

Wyatt's face grew grimmer as Ramsay spoke. When he was done, Wyatt leaned over to give Beatrice a quick hug.

"I'm fine now," she said with a smile. "I'm just glad it's over and that Sterling has been taken to jail."

"Where he'll be for a long, long time," added Ramsay sternly. "Well, I'm going to leave you folks and head on home to face the music with Meadow for not making it to the quilt show."

"I think she'd absolve you when you tell her you've put the murderer behind bars," said Beatrice wryly. "Besides, there'll be other quilt shows."

"That's one thing I've learned. There will *always* be other quilt shows," said Ramsay with a chuckle.

After he left, Wyatt and Beatrice sat quietly together on the sofa for a few minutes, Beatrice softly rubbing Noo-noo.

"Here's what I'm thinking," said Wyatt slowly. "Tomorrow morning, we'll have a repeat of the breakfast I made before all this started."

"Scrambled eggs, sausage, and pancakes?" asked Beatrice, perking up a little.

"Exactly. Except, instead of having them outside, I'll bring you breakfast in bed," said Wyatt with a smile.

"That sounds like the perfect way to start a new day," said Beatrice, reaching over the corgi to give Wyatt a hug.

About the Author:

Elizabeth writes the Southern Quilting mysteries and Memphis Barbeque mysteries for Penguin Random House and the Myrtle Clover series for Midnight Ink and independently. She blogs at ElizabethSpannCraig.com/blog, named by Writer's Digest as one of the 101 Best Websites for Writers. Elizabeth makes her home in Matthews, North Carolina, with her husband. She's the mother of two.

Sign up for Elizabeth's free newsletter to stay updated on releases:

https://bit.ly/2xZUXqO

This and That

I love hearing from my readers. You can find me on Facebook as Elizabeth Spann Craig Author, on Twitter as elizabethscraig, on my website at elizabethspanncraig.com, and by email at elizabethspanncraig@gmail.com.

Thanks so much for reading my book...I appreciate it. If you enjoyed the story, would you please leave a short review on the site where you purchased it? Just a few words would be great. Not only do I feel encouraged reading them, but they also help other readers discover my books. Thank you!

Did you know my books are available in print and ebook formats? And most of the Myrtle Clover series is available in audio. Find them on Audible or iTunes.

Please follow me on BookBub for book recommendations and release notifications: https://www.bookbub.com/profile/elizabeth-spann-craig .

I have Myrtle Clover tote bags, charms, magnets, and other goodies at my Café Press shop: https://www.cafepress.com/cozymystery

If you'd like an autographed book for yourself or a friend, please visit my Etsy page.

I'd also like to thank some folks who helped me put this book together. Thanks to my cover designer, Karri Klawiter, for her awesome covers. Thanks to my editor, Judy Beatty, for all of her help. Thanks to beta readers Amanda Arrieta and Dan Harris for all of their helpful suggestions and careful reading. Thanks, as always, to my family and readers.

A special thanks to John DeMeo for his support on Patreon!

Other Works by the Author:

Myrtle Clover Series in Order (be sure to look for the Myrtle series in audio, ebook, and print):

Pretty is as Pretty Dies
Progressive Dinner Deadly
A Dyeing Shame
A Body in the Backyard
Death at a Drop-In
A Body at Book Club
Death Pays a Visit
A Body at Bunco
Murder on Opening Night
Cruising for Murder
Cooking is Murder
A Body in the Trunk
Cleaning is Murder
Edit to Death
Hushed Up
A Body in the Attic
Murder on the Ballot (late 2020)

Southern Quilting Mysteries in Order:

Quilt or Innocence
Knot What it Seams
Quilt Trip
Shear Trouble
Tying the Knot
Patch of Trouble
Fall to Pieces
Rest in Pieces
On Pins and Needles
Fit to be Tied
Embroidering the Truth
Knot a Clue

The Village Library Mysteries in Order:

Checked Out
Overdue
Borrowed Time
Hush-Hush (late 2020)

Memphis Barbeque Mysteries in Order (Written as Riley Adams):

Delicious and Suspicious
Finger Lickin' Dead
Hickory Smoked Homicide
Rubbed Out

And a standalone "cozy zombie" novel: Race to Refuge, written as Liz Craig

CPSIA information can be obtained
at www.ICGtesting.com
Printed in the USA
BVHW041958020920
587791BV00004B/103